The Strange Case of William Whipper-Snapper

All the very best for the future

Be happy

- David -

David R Morgan

David R Morgan

The Strange Case of William Whipper-Snapper

This is a work of fiction.

Library of Congress Control Number: 2020917834

Printed in the United States of America

A 2 Z Press LLC

PO Box 582

Deleon Springs, FL 32130

bestlittleonlinebookstore.com

sizemore3630@aol.com

440-241-3126

ISBN: 978-1-946908-62-9

DEDICATION:

*This is for my dad and mum,
without whom none of this would
have been possible;
for Bex and Toby who are the magic in my life
and to Sue, for all her love and
support through so many years...
and for Master William Whipper-Snapper,
my secret friend and great-grandson
of William - a case in point.
One must always expect the unexpected.*

Contents

1

How It All Began

This story, or so I have been told by someone whose words I have no reason to doubt, is a true tale. It involves many weird and rather wonderful happenings - at least 'I' think they are wonderful - and I am sure that after you have read of William Whipper-Snapper's strange case you will think so as well.

Now, when it all began, Master William Whipper-Snapper was fourteen years old and as troublesome and mischievous as anyone ever has been. His sister Emma was ten and, although the golden orange of her mother's affections, seeming so, so well behaved, she was in fact as mischievous as William was.

It should be said that William and Emma had only one thing in common and that was their hearty dislike for each other. One was always trying to annoy the other. William usually ending up with the blame as Emma was unusually proficient at acting the innocent and telling tales.

As you can imagine, Dr. and Mrs. Whipper-Snapper had quite a hard time controlling their children when they were together. Dr. Henry Whipper-Snapper had no time for 'tomfoolery,' being a well-respected country doctor who always appeared to have too much on his mind. He believed in the seriousness of life. A very cautious man, he only ever smiled an inch at a time. Now, Mrs. Emily Whipper-Snapper was quite the opposite of her husband. She loved pictures, poetry, and the comedy of politics that seemed to her like a hilarious 'men's only' party; which made little sense.

Ah! But enough of this. What year was it when it all began? I hear you say. Quite right too. It was in the time of Our Lord 1880 when Queen Victoria was on her Throne of England, Great Britain, the Commonwealth, the Empire, etc. Yes, and she had been since 1837.

Almost every Victorian Gentleman wore a beard or moustache or muttonchops, or even like Dr. Whipper-Snapper, all three. Victorian ladies wore crinolines or bustles and, like Mrs. Whipper-Snapper when she got the chance, extravagant hats. And Children? Well, children should be seen and not heard, though William was more often than not heard very, very loudly, and nowhere to be seen when he was wanted. Whenever his mother told him to be quiet William would tease her by chanting, "Speak when spoken to, put time to useful employ; shut the door after you, good little boy!" This either made her laugh or cross, depending on her mood.

Now, talking of moods brings us to the precise time that we are talking about, the Christmas holiday; in fact only seven days before Christmas itself. William, as we know, was at home. What hasn't been said was that during term time he resided at Josiah's Blisset's Boarding School for Refined Young Gentlemen. Now, I could tell you tales of William's pranks at school, where Dr. Blisset reigned like a cross between Atila the Hun and plum pudding. Tales such as the time when William asked his teacher Ebenezer Crusher if he could be punished for something he hadn't done.

"Of course, not Whipper-Snapper." replied the worthy.

"Oh good, Sir," William said happily. "Because I haven't done what you asked me to do. I was too busy puzzling out why a raven is like a writing desk. Is it something to do with the wings?"

Or the time when William put frogspawn in Dr. Blisset's raspberry jam and the good fellow complained of soggy toast. But these are not part of the story, so I won't rattle on.

William's mischievousness at school had however caused a tricky scene when his father had read his report. It conveyed in Mr. Blissett's own elaborate handwriting the good fellow's obvious dismay.

"His term project is both good and original. However, where it is original, it is not good and where it is good, it is not original. The improvement in the legibility of his handwriting is beginning to reveal great deficiencies in his spelling. He is intelligent but unwilling to work at anything except mischief. Something must be done to curb his behavior." And so on.

After having sent William to bed with a sore backside from seven strokes of a slipper, Dr. Whipper-Snapper said to his wife, "Well! I can see what William will be when he learns anything useful."

"What Henry dear?"

"An old man," was the bitter reply.

However, with the approach of Yuletide and the decorating of the Christmas tree, his mother had quite forgotten William's bad behavior. Even his father seemed to have forgotten him a little; for the time being! Though he said several times to William, "You are going to have to learn boy, that in this life you must often borrow from tomorrow to pay your debts of yesterday."

'Whatever that means!' thought William, as no doubt you may; though William would soon see how tomorrow could indeed affect yesterday.

But to return to how it all began.

See the house; fairly large, with a conservatory at one side. A typical Victorian country house.

Now, go across the croquet lawn to the new summer

house, enter through the front door into the tidy hall, and go down to the kitchen. Here, William watches old Martha the cook, preparing a large brandy fruitcake after having spiced the thick orange marmalade.

"Looks very good, doesn't it, Vizit?" William spoke to what seemed like empty air, but to William, Vizit was his invisible partner in pranks.

"Lor bless I, you, and yourn foolishness," Old Martha laughed. William caught a large dollop of rich cake mixture that oozed off the bottom of her expansive wooden stirring spoon.

"Ummm. It does taste rather nice, Martha. Vizit says that you're definitely improving."

"Cheeky rascal. Be off with yourn. You don't stick at nothing teasing. I can't be doing with it." But both her fat red cheeks bobbed like a happy balloon, tethered at either end of her wide smile. William liked Martha. He had known her for as long as he could recall. He remembered the stories she had told him of the Old Man in the Moon and his unusual meals.

She went back to her stirring. Laughing, William dipped his finger in the bowl. He felt the sticky, velvety mixture congeal around his finger as he scooped it up to his mouth.

"Oh do go on, be off with yourn. There's some must be working and you should be at some this very moment as is I daresay." She put on mock annoyance.

"What do you say to that proposal Vizit? Should we 'be off'?'" He flicked a tiny globule of the mixture from the table onto Martha's neck.

"Dirty monkey." She raised her spoon threateningly. "I wish as I knew what to do with yourn, but seeing as I don't, I won't this time! Joost be off."

Laughing, William wandered out of the kitchen. Not because he had been told to; oh no, rather because he was bored with teasing Martha and uncooked cake mixture never did taste as good as it should.

Dr. Blisset said that the little William knew he owed to his ignorance and that his want of knowledge must be the result of years of study. But William did like certain things, especially history and mythology. William would have liked to have had good results for his lessons, but really, it just seemed like too much work and he couldn't be bothered with all that. He wanted what he wanted as soon as he wanted it; and why not? He reasoned the world would be a much happier place if everyone could have all their wishes fulfilled at once, without having to waste time on any work.

William meandered into the drawing room. His mother was embroidering a cushion with red and white roses set amongst a twine of green stems and leaves. William could never understand why she seemed so devoted to stitching beauty into something that people would merely use for sitting on.

"Good morning, William," his mother said without looking up from her occupation.

"Good morning, Mama," he answered casually. "Have they cut down the old oak yet?"

"I don't think so, William." His mother still didn't raise her head. "Mr. Cleathorpe and Mr. Harris are still hard at work."

William idly picked up an apple from the large silver bowl on the sideboard, took one bite, and deciding that he couldn't be bothered to eat anymore; he put it back in such a way so as to disguise the fact that it had been touched by teeth. Yawning, he scratched his dark curly hair and went over to the French window.

Outside, across the lawn, he could see Tom the gardener and Bob the handyman busily working the large teeth of a big two-handed saw deep into the bark of the old tree.

The oak was at least three hundred years old.

Although it was still alive, for some reason its roots had become progressively looser and looser until the whole tree swayed dangerously in the most moderate of winds. If it fell down by itself, it might very well land on the new summerhouse. So, Tom and Bob had fastened ropes around it, securing them with 'guys' to the ground and were cutting through its huge trunk in such a way that it would land harmlessly on the flower garden that was lying fallow during the winter. The two men were, however, obviously encountering some difficulty.

The sky was brewing heavy weather. A tumbling wind was whistling around the two men, foreshadowing an oncoming storm. William wished that this meant snow. He loved snow. He had been hoping for it for days.

Then he saw his father, beard and muttonchops as black as raven's wings, stride across the croquet lawn to see how the work was progressing. He was wearing his long blue-grey overcoat and his Billycock hat. William thought that these made his father look rather like an officer.

The men stopped their sawing as he started to talk about something with them. They talked. They looked at the tree. They talked some more.

William wished the tree would come down easily and quickly. It was then, almost as if responding to his thought, that a tremendous gust of wind rattled the windows, lifted some tiles off the roof, and made William's mother look up from her embroidery. The gust caught the tree by the neck and pulled it up from its place; breaking the holding ropes, cracking the bark, and wrenching up the roots. Then the wind heaved heavy shoulders against the tree.

"What's happening?" Emma rushed into the room.

The wind pushed the tree like a piston pushing iron.

"Emma, don't run. It isn't lady-like."

"Sorry, Mama, but what is happening? I saw the tree swaying from my bedroom window."

The wind heaved one last time.

William didn't take any notice of his sister. He rushed past her and ran outside.

"Look out, Papa," he screamed.

But the three men were standing as though hypnotised, held like statues by the tree, which leant right over and began to fall.

William wished the tree would come down easily and quickly.

"Look out, papa!" William screamed.

2

Roots To The Case

The crash was sickening to hear. With a tremendous 'bang,' the tree smashed through the roof of the new summer house; only coming to rest after it had practically split the building in two.

"Goodness!" Emma gasped.

"Dear, oh dear, oh dear," Mrs. Whipper-Snapper, who had joined the children outside, kept repeating, like a musical box stuck on one particular note.

William felt like laughing. Not because if you looked at the situation in a certain way it was funny, but because none of the three men had been hurt by the tree's downfall. Also, another factor cheered him.

"It's beginning to snow!" he declared happily. The flakes were large and dry. They would certainly settle.

"Come inside children. Let your Papa work things out with the men." She had a sigh in her voice.

"Oh, Mama, please let me see if I can help," William pleaded.

"You never help anyone," Emma snapped.

"Shut up *little* child," William retorted.

"Now, now you two." Their mother just wanted some peace. She wondered how on earth they were going to pay for the repairs.

"If you put your coat on William, you can go out for a little while."

They went inside. Mrs. Whipper-Snapper sat down in the drawing room again.

"Vizit says you're a booby," William said to his sister, knowing how it irked her when he used Vizit's name. You see Vizit was originally Emma's invisible playmate, but William had taken the name to annoy her and anyone else he could. Emma resisted the temptation to be really cross. She simply stuck her tongue out at him.

Incensed, William grabbed hold of the offending object. He gave it a sharp tug.

She tried to cry out but found it impossible with her brother still firmly grasping her tongue. By the time he had let go and she went crying to their mother, William had his coat on and jaunted outside.

He rushed over to where the three men were checking the extent of the damage.

"Now keep out of the way boy," his father gravely waved him aside.

"But Papa!" William protested.

"I'm jiggered if it's not always the way," his father muttered. "The one thing I didn't want to happen has." He was too busy moaning to listen to William.

The wind was whirling snowflakes into hanging white spiral chains in the frosty air. It was coming down so hard now that it was beginning to be difficult to see.

"Joost look at 'em critters. They're fair mixing it Doctor," said Old Tom. "Mebbies 'twould b' best if yourn leave it ta me and Mr. 'Arris 'ere."

"Yes. Yes, Cleathorpe. It is getting rather too thick for comfort. Discretion the better part of valour and all that." He turned and started towards the house with long striding steps.

"Come on," he called to William impatiently.

William grunted, "Yes Papa," begrudgingly, and followed.

"Dear, dear," his father kept saying to himself. "It's going to cost a great deal; a great deal. Still, *nil desperandum* I suppose."

They trudged in together as the wind continued to whistle almost mockingly outside.

For the rest of the day, it snowed so heavily that even Tom and Mr. Harris had to leave off working. Emma, still complaining about her sore tongue, helped her mother dress the Christmas tree and William, well William didn't help anyone.

By the next morning, the snow had ceased. Frost crystals sparkled on the window glass in the cold early sun.

The William was wide-awake and up and out well before breakfast. Only his father was up before him. Dr. Whipper-Snapper had gone out on a house call to Mrs. Grabber-Williams, whose varicose veins always played up at the most inconvenient times.

The snow had settled exactly as William had hoped it would; crisp and deep and even. As he waded through, it covered his shoes and the bottom of his trousers. He went towards the disaster area of the fallen tree, which was lying quite contentedly amidst the rubble and broken glass.

Kicking the snow off his feet, William climbed onto the thick old trunk. He gazed around. His mischievous eyes fixed on the roots that sprawled like long brown fingers pointing upwards at something invisible in the air. He crept closer to the earthy hand. What really caught his attention was a particularly large root that bent over and extended down into the snow-covered ground, just as if it was being held by something.

William tightrope walked on the trunk to the webbed network of roots. He attempted to pull the large root up. It was definitely weighted down, entangled in something.

11

He jumped down to explore further.

As he landed in the white covering above the churned-up earth, he was sure that he heard a groan. He pulled. The root was well stuck. He tugged. It wouldn't budge. Even so, for once William didn't give up. Something made him feel that he must go on pulling, until - "Stop it you!" The voice was educated, if rather high-pitched.

William stepped back, very surprised. To make sure he wasn't just hearing things, he gave the root another sharp jerk.

"Stop that you!" the voice exclaimed. "Stop that, do you hear! You'll negate my Droopsfier; even unwind my gyrating Domwangler!"

"Who said that?" William craned his neck. "Is that you, Emma being your usual foolish self?" He looked round for any sign of his sister. There was none.

"Don't 'you' be foolish. I am a 1.B. Prize. Move some earth and you will see me, dumbo!"

William jumped back. He was certain now that the voice was coming from the earth just beneath his feet, or somewhere near.

"Where....whereabouts are you exactly?" he said, kicking some of the snow away.

"Under the earth, clodhopper!"

'Really!' William thought. Whatever it is, it's certainly very rude. He gazed at the root once more.

"This earth?" He pointed at the root.

"For goodness sake. I could spend the rest of eternity having this conversation! Just move some earth, buffalo!" The voice was impatient.

"Alright, alright." William kicked aside the remainder of the snow. The upheaval of the tree had left a deep hollow, with just a surface crust of loose earth that caved in at William's first attempt at digging.

"Careful!" the voice nagged. "You'll squash my Somniscope!"

"Yes, quite!" William wondered what sort of thing could go on and on so, using such strange words.

The earth was very cold. William had forgotten his gloves. He kept blowing hot breath on his hands to stop them from freezing up.

"Now that's more like it my lad," the voice said approvingly.

However, it seemed to William that all he was uncovering was more and more of the root.

"It goes on forever," William complained.

"Just like you! Can't see for looking. Space is curved and I should know. Nothing is endless as such." The voice was pompous. "Though some say being is born of not being."

"If you say so." William restrained a note of total bewilderment. His hands were beginning to feel like ice-lollies. But it was strange, he thought, that he didn't find this situation really unusual. That is until he finally found out what was at the end of the root.

The root had entwined itself through what appeared to be some form of shiny silver case. "Shake a leg dumbo," it said. "Get me up."

William jumped away. "Are….are you in….inside?" William was confused.

"Well, you could say that. And you have," the voice replied dryly. "Now stop dithering. Lift me out will you!"

William crept forward cautiously. He bent down. The case was silver all over, being about the size and thickness of a small book. On the front of it was what seemed like a little purple button, on which was inscribed in silver, "1.B."

William pulled the root away from around the case, which, having been slightly open all this time, suddenly snapped shut. Tentatively and rather apprehensively, William lifted it out. It was really quite light for its size.

"Don't be as jumpy as a squirrel," the case cautioned. "Careless hands make lost opportunity."

13

"Uh?" William was dumbfounded. The voice seemed not to be coming from inside the case, but from the case itself.

"Still confused, are we?" the case said.

"Well, a….a little." William was totally bewildered.

"William, what are you doing over there boy? Come in at once." The voice was all-too-familiar - his father's bellow. He had just returned from his house call. William hurriedly hid the case beneath his coat.

"I'm coming Papa," William shouted.

"Well come in at once. Stop your stuff and nonsense. Breakfast will be served soon." Turning, his father stomped moodily inside.

"Oh, fudge!" William sighed.

"Don't let that bother you, sonny," the case said. "I'm a 1.B. Prize and I'm yours. You must use me soon. I need exercising, understand?"

"Look, please be quiet for a while. I have to go inside and Papa's in a grumpy enough mood as it is." William anxiously walked towards the house. "I don't want anyone to know about you," he added. "Why I don't even know what you are or what you do yet."

"You will," the case said. "Oh yes, you certainly will."

As the snow began again, falling like frozen apple blossom onto the white carpeted ground, William wondered what on earth he had let himself in for.

3

Change For The Worse

William cast his gaze around to make sure that the hall was empty.

"Use me soon. Use me soon." The case was being irksomely loud.

"Yes, alright! I will. I will. But I must have my breakfast first." William tried to keep a pleading tone out of his voice.

"Okey-dokey. But remember you stomach-minded individual, my Domwangler needs gyrating. After all, you idle creature, I have been snarked for some time. Eh!"

"I don't know what you're talking about! Just please 'shush' for a moment or they'll hear you."

"Hear, schmear," the case said bitterly.

William took his coat off carefully, so as to keep the case concealed. Walking past the morning room, he could see his father, mother, and sister at the breakfast table. His mother was saying something about the cost of repairs. Emma was eating too much as usual, although she was as thin as a ruler, and his father was reading his copy of *The Times* that had been warmed to freshness in the kitchen range by Walters the housemaid.

'A piping hot *Times* on a cold winter's day is as valuable

15

as a well-kept vow' was one of Dr. Whipper-Snapper's popular adages.

Walters emerged from downstairs. She was as close as a clam and as bald as a boiled egg, apart from a fringe of stiff black hair that formed a dark halo around her cap. Being absurdly persnickety, William always thought Walters probably even asked the sun to wipe its feet before it came in in the morning.

"Didn't you hear your parents call you into breakfast, Master William? Henderson served it long ago," she said. She was carrying a bundle of sheets.

"What's that shiny thing under your coat?" She moved towards him.

"Mind your own business," snapped the case.

"Shh. Be quiet," William urged.

"Cheeky young scamp," Walters said angrily.

William attempted to push the case further into the folds of his coat, but she came right up to him.

William attempted to push the case further into the folds of his coat but she came right up to him. Putting down the bundle of sheets, she put her hand in the coat and brought out the case.

"What's this?" She held up the case. "It's not yours, is it? Where did you get this box from?"

"Your ignorance is proverbial," the case said indignantly. "I'm no 'box,' I'm a 1.B. Prize!"

Walters jumped back startled, letting the case drop. Luckily, it landed on the coat, not the floor.

"You're chronically stupid," the case complained. "You could have deranged my Droopsifier."

"William," his mother called out, "what is all that noise? Your father told you to come to the table a long time ago. Now come at once."

Walters flashed William a look of indignant confusion mixed with intense anger. She turned in a flustered huff and scurried noisily off, with her bundle of sheets. "Good riddance," the case said.

William couldn't help smiling.

As he approached the morning room, William heard his father say, "That boy can never do what he is told. He will make all our hair go grey. The sooner he goes back to school the better."

William could hear Emma still complaining about her tongue.

"Pah!" William moaned. Unconsciously his finger strayed onto the case's little purple button. The case opened a little.

"I wish they would all change," he muttered to himself, "and be more like me."

"Ah, fantabulosa! That's more like it! My Somniscope is as fine as the day it was first installed," the case said luxuriantly, shutting itself.

Not listening, William hid the case again. "Please be quiet will you. I'm in enough trouble already." He hung his coat on the large wooden hallstand and hurried into breakfast.

Suddenly, there was a crash from inside the room. As soon as he entered, his sister jumped up and kissed him affectionately on the cheek. William was very shocked, but he was even more taken aback to see his mother balancing a very soft-boiled egg on the tip of her nose and his father wearing a paper crown made from *The Times*. His father giggled and proceeded to attempt to stick a chipolata sausage up his right nostril, for no apparent reason at all.

"W...what is happening?" William gasped.

"This, podsnap," his father guffawed, and threw the sausage at his wife, hitting the egg, which broke and split its contents over her face. William let out a quiet laugh. It was funny to see such things. He soon stopped, however, when he saw another sausage coming his way at considerable speed.

Before he could duck, it hit him right in the left eye.

"Crimney, that hurt!" he cried out in pain, holding a hand over the afflicted area.

"Naughty, naughty," Mrs. Whipper-Snapper chuckled and threw an uneaten plate of scrambled eggs straight into her husband's inanely smirking face. He jumped up like a Jack-in-the-Box and danced a Horn-Pipe Jig.

All this time, Emma had been watching the ludicrous antics with very great disapproval.

"Papa! Mama!" she cried out angrily. "Manners! You really must learn how to behave!" As she went up to her father, she shook a reprimanding finger. With a giggle and a twirl, he poured lukewarm coffee all over her head. He immediately slumped into his seat, clutching his belly as he laughed uncontrollably.

"Well really!" Emma yelled. Taking his paper crown, she tore it up into little pieces.

"Tore my crown, you tore my crown! And I was king of the castle, you nasty little rascal." He started crying.

William felt that he was a spectator in some absurd pantomime.

"I just don't believe it. What possibly could have caused this?" he pondered anxiously.

"You," said a voice from the hall.

"Me?" William just managed to sidestep out of the Kamikaze path of a willow pattern plate, which smashed against the wall next to him. "Me?" he said again as he hurried into the hall and grabbed his coat down from the stand. He took out the case.

"Yes 'you,' dumbo," said the case.

Just then, Walters, wearing some sort of crazy bright blue wig, whirled into the hall singing and knocked William flat on his back.

"Well really! This is all just too much to bear!" William snapped. He got up feeling that it *was* all just too much to bear.

18

"I think that you caused this," he said angrily to the case.

"Don't be so tiresome," the case replied testily. "You wished it. To err is human; to be wrong is not part of Company policy."

"Oh, very well." William thought as quickly as he could under the circumstances. "Now I wish...."

"First you must press my purple Domwangler button to activate my Sominiscope," the case interrupted.

"Alright, alright." But before William could even put his finger on the button, Walters spun by again. She grabbed the case and jumped away.

"Hey!" William yelled. "Stop that! Give it back!"

"Yes, unhand me you repulsive bacon-rasher!" cried the case indignantly.

Too late! Walters pirouetted about and went ballet dancing down into the kitchen.

A coffee cup came crashing out from the breakfast-room and landed in a shower of china at William's feet. Ignoring this, the desperate boy ran after the deranged housemaid to the kitchen.

"Eh, joost what dya want, ya yoong brat," Martha growled in a most aggressive accent. Her face was incredibly red with anger. Grabbing a large wooden rolling pin, she trundled towards him like a deadly tram hysterically out of control.

"Oh, crimney!" William gasped. He dashed behind the large kitchen table for protection. He was about to say something to reason with Martha when the rolling pin came curving round to give him a resounding 'slap' on the backside.

Meanwhile, Walters, who was still dancing, had somehow managed to open the case.

"I wish. I wish. I wish," she kept repeating in a singsong voice when suddenly the case snapped shut. With a grunt of dismay, she attempted to bite it open.

"Hey! Stop that, mush-mouth!" the case howled.

There was the alarming sound of a heavy crash from upstairs.

Old Martha lunged once more at William with her destructive weapon. Out of pure distilled desperation, William ran. He took a flying leap at the twirling Walters and grabbed the case from out of her mouth.

"You took your time," the case complained.

William ignored the remark. Both Old Martha and Walters were closing in on him. Hurriedly, he pressed the button. The case opened. For the first time, he noticed the soft purple light that glowed from within it.

"I wish for everything to become normal again."

"Why not!" the case replied.

Like waking from a crazy dream, William was back in the hall just as he had been before he had inadvertently made the wish.

"Thank goodness," William sighed with relief.

"Henry! What on earth has happened?"

It was his mother's startled voice and by the sound of it, William could tell that the trouble was not nearly over yet.

4

Looking a Gift Horse in the Mouth

William walked apprehensively into the room and immediately wished that he could walk out again unnoticed. The scene was an utter shambles. There was coffee, sausages, and eggs all over the place, though mainly over the three people who were looking around, mouths agape, and expressions blank.

William slid back into the hall. He took the case from his coat.

"Now look here," he began, "I said bring things back to normal."

"Quite so, old chap," the case replied. "I made your family change as requested and, as requested, I changed them back. What they did during the time of their change is none of my business. I won't interfere. Really, what do you expect – miracles?"

"William, come here immediately, boy." His father's voice sounded furious.

Hiding the case, William went back into the room, rather sheepishly.

"Are you responsible for all this...this..." his father sputtered, waving his hands around the room in great agitation, "this, this chaos?"

"No, Papa."

"Yes, he is," Emma said tearfully gazing at the coffee stains on her dress.

"But I'm not!" William protested.

"Go to your room immediately, boy," his father boomed.

"But Papa."

"GO."

William saw that there was simply no reasoning with them. His mother still seemed somewhat stunned by it all, though a vague smile played around her lips. So, hangdog, he got his coat, went to his room, and shut the door crossly behind him.

"For a moment," William said to himself, "I was hoping I had imagined it all."

"Course not," said the case bluntly. "I am a Grade 1.B. Prize. Only Grade 2.B. Prizes produce illusions. I have a synchronized Droopsifier and Somniscope to create forms of reality upon request."

"But crimney! I didn't ask you to make everything go bonkers!"

"You wished things to change and they did, didn't they?" the case stated. "Really, nothing is enough for some people to whom enough is not enough."

"But...oh, what's the use!" William experienced a sinking feeling. He lay on his stomach on the bed, with the case in front of him.

"Well, ok....what are you really?" he said at last.

"Don't be ridiculous – I'm a 1.B. Prize."

"Yes, so you've said." William tried not to feel too irritated. "But *what* are you really?"

"I know what I'm not."

"What?"

"I'm not...going to tell you what I am! Prizes are forbidden to be personal. The Great Prize-Maker has a patent

22

pending and wishes, therefore, to keep the process of creation a secret."

"I see!" William didn't see at all. "Well then, where do you come from? and who is this 'Great Prize-Maker?'"

"I originate from Theomodor. And the Great Prize-Maker is the Great Prize-Maker."

"Where is Theomodor? What country is it in?"

"If you don't know, then I can't tell you."

"Crimney, this is simply getting me nowhere, except back to the beginning again and now I don't know where to begin at all."

"To be a success, one must know when to begin anything and when to stop anything," the case said pompously.

"Oh, alright," William began, "if you are, as you say, my Prize now, then why are you mine and what exactly can you do?"

"I grant wishes, as I thought you would have gathered by now. I was given to your family and, as you are the first-born of your generation to find me, I am now yours. Mind you, puffball, if that root hadn't touched my Domwangler, I would never have been able to bring the tree down. Terrible! You might never have found me. Yes, I don't know how long I was underground but I'm sure that there wasn't any tree above me at first. And yes, by Jove, I do believe there was another building where this house now stands."

"Goodness, that oak must be hundreds of years old! I do remember reading once of another house on this site centuries ago. Don't know why it came down though. Really, it is very hard to understand the meaning of any of this."

"You are meant to use me, not to understand me; that isn't important," the case stressed. "Make another request, and for pity's sake try to think this time."

William found the case considerably irksome when it talked in this bossy fashion. Even so, his curiosity had been

23

firmly aroused again, but he wanted time to ponder what to ask for.

"It's wonderful how shiny you still are after all those years underground," he said stalling for time.

"Don't dwell on trivia. Make a request." The case was most empathetic.

"Oh, alright. I....I wish you had a sense of humor," he said pressing the button. *He'd show that case!*

"Ever heard the one about the well?" the case asked suddenly.

"No."

"Too deep for you? Ha-ha. You know the story of the clouds?"

"No, but..."

"Way above your head. Ha-ha ha."

"Listen," William began, "I didn't mean...."

"Do you know the song about the red-hot poker?" William just scowled angrily.

"You'd never grasp it," laughed the case. "Ha-ha, haha."

"I wish you would stop," huffed William.

"What do you think I am, buffo! I wasn't granting a request. I thought I would just illustrate how unnecessary a sense of humor is. A 1.B. Prize is a serious thing, only Grade 3 Prizes are comedians. Now, kindly make a proper request. I might as well be under the tree for the amount of good you're doing me!"

William thought this is a very curious way for a Prize to be looking at things.

"I can make any wish and you will grant it?" he asked.

"Within reason. Only 1.A. Specials have unlimited Domwanglers. Think yourself lucky to have a Grade 1.B., my lad!"

"Yes, quite!"

Now William had had a strong yearning for one thing, though his father had told him that he couldn't have one until his schoolwork showed a radical improvement. So, he had never been given one.

William pressed the button. The case opened. He couldn't see anything inside, for a deep purple light shone out strongly, creating a barrier of color.

"I wish I had a fine horse, all my own," he said.

"I know two things about a horse, and one of them is rather coarse," the case said in a satisfied voice.

At once there was the sound of proud, loud neighing from outside.

William jumped up and rushed to his window just in time to witness a large white stallion, glorious in the snow, galloping around the finely kept croquet lawn. It was happily churning up snow and grass under hoof.

Like a worried crab, Old Tom came scurrying up to the horse waving his arms in horror at the damage being done.

"Ere, you joost stop't. Curs'ed critter," he cried out. But suddenly he halted and was silent. The stallion turned about and charged at the poor fellow. Old Tom, moving faster than he had done for the past twenty years, managed to escape being trampled six feet under by jumping behind the remains of the summer house.

"What the deuce is all this kerfuffle, Cleathorpe? What's that horse doing on my croquet lawn?" Dr. Whipper-Snapper shouted, flabbergasted, as he ran out of the conservatory. Oblivious, the horse continued on its destructive course.

"Sure I joost doon't know sir," said poor Old Tom, still crouching behind rubble.

"Oh, no. No!" William gasped. "You've done it again." He hurried over and grabbed the case.

"I wished for a horse to ride." The case opened. "To ride, not to....."

Before he could finish what he was saying, William found himself outside, astride the bounding white steed. His father was staring aghast at his son's sudden appearance atop the creature.

"What on earth are you doing, boy?" he yelled, anger surmounting surprise. But William was too busy hanging on for dear life itself to give any sensible answer. And, even if he hadn't been, how could he possibly explain this away!

The horse reared and raced towards the ruins beside the fallen oak. Tom sprawled himself flat on the ground. The horse hurdled him by several feet.

"Help!" William screamed. "Somebody help me!"

The horse pirouetted about, erect on its two hind legs, and then charged towards Dr. Whipper-Snapper at full gallop, kicking a drift of snow over Old Tom as he did so.

Everything flashed by William's fearful gaze until the horse seemed to literally jump at his bewildered father and William was bucked off high into the air. He felt the case in his hand; quickly he pressed the button.

"I wish I had never wished for a horse."

His eyes were shut tight. Instead of landing with a thud on the ground, he landed lightly on his bed.

"I think it's disgusting," the case complained to the stunned boy, "I wish you would make up your mind what it is you want. I really can't go on 'unwishing' things. It's bad for me, might even overload my Droopsifier!"

William didn't know what to say or feel. Getting things exactly when you wanted them wasn't such fun after all.

Suddenly, "My lawn, my lovely croquet lawn," a loud voice proclaimed.

William winced. He went over to the window, feeling like a joke with no punchline. The lawn was a terrible mess.

"It's still churned up! All churned up!" William failed to restrain a strong note of despair in his voice. "You didn't change it back."

"Course not, dumbo," the case replied indignantly. "It's a question of cause and effect, mind over matter. I can cause the cause upon request, but the effect is out of my control. I'm forbidden to interfere."

"What about the mind over matter?" William asked disheartened.

"Oh, merely, gopher, that as far as I'm concerned I don't mind causing anything because it doesn't matter to me."

William groaned. This 'Prize' was becoming as handy as a headache.

His mother called from downstairs. Anxious about everything, William put the case away, despite its protests. He placed it in the top draw of his trunk and went tentatively downstairs.

The mess in the breakfast room had been largely cleared up by the maids, although Walters gave him a most peculiar look as she sauntered past.

Luckily, Williams found that his parents had decided to give him the benefit of the doubt, despite Emma's protests. Besides, his father was now totally preoccupied with an incredulous Tom and Mr. Harris attempting to discern 'what the devil has happened to the lawn.'

After lunch, pretending to do some work, William went back to his room. One good thing was that no one except him seemed to remember the change or the antics of the white horse; all they witnessed were the effects.

"Ah, we're back. Took our time didn't we!" the case said bitterly as William brought it out. William just stared at it for a moment.

"Well, I'm not going to fritter my wits on you," snapped the case. "Just make a request – pronto."

"No."

"Please don't say that word! Press my Domwangler immediately."

But William put the case back and went downstairs again. He went into the playroom wondering what was to be done if every request he made would go wrong. He just couldn't chance any more mistakes.

27

Emma walked in, holding a handful of celandines she had gathered outside. William cast a baleful look at her. She returned a surly gaze.

"There's a funny noise coming from your bedroom," she said. "I tried to see what it was, but you've locked the door. Why?"

"None of your business. Don't go poking your nose in where it shouldn't be or the Man in the Moon will change it into a fat pork sausage and cook it for his supper."

"Don't be so horrid!" she said and stomped out.

After she was gone, William went back to his room to investigate. Even before he opened the door, he could hear, "Domwangler, Domwangler, Domwangler," repeated over and over again.

"That case!" William walked in very disgruntled. He took the case out.

"I don't mean a thing to you, do I? Not a jot!" the case said sorrowfully. "It's not right that you should put me away in the dark now that I'm yours."

William conceded reluctantly to staying in his room reading for the rest of the day, though he refused to make another request despite the case's constant nagging.

That night he slept very uneasily – the case insisted on waking him up to ask if he'd got to sleep yet. The truth was that the case was lonely. The case always wished to make its presence felt, like an over-eager and slightly worrying puppy....a puppy with haywire 'magical' powers!

Despite his bad night, William felt slightly better in the morning. It had started snowing once more.

"Come on then, sleepy-head," the case urged. "Make a request. I've been patient so far, but enough is enough."

Yes, William agreed, enough is enough. "Look," he said, "I don't know what to request."

"Don't be an ignoramus; activate my Somniscope," the case snapped.

"What are you doing, Billy?" a scornful voice said. "Talking to Vizit again?"

William turned with a cringe. Emma had entered his room unnoticed.

"I'm doing nothing, you scrawny pest," he said.

"Oh, yes you are." She moved closer. "What's that you're holding?"

"None of your business." He tried to conceal the case.

"It isn't yours!" she said.

"Yes, I am, butter-brain!" the case said emphatically.

"Who said that?" Emma scanned around.

"I did, cuckoo-head," snapped the case.

"Be quiet," William hissed to the case. "It was me, Emma. Now please go away."

"Oh no, you didn't speak," she insisted.

"Top marks, you glimmering booby," the case snapped.

"Go away." William gave her a sharp push.

"I'll tell Mama," Emma said, "and Papa; then you'll be in real trouble. Just you wait and see."

"Oh, for goodness sake, Emma, you little beast."

"No," she said firmly.

William eyed his sister resentfully. She pouted her lips, toyed with her chestnut curls of hair, met his gaze, and adamantly refused to budge. He knew how proud she was of the fact that she was pretty and like most pretty people, to be called ugly is a severe blow to their morale.

"You're so ugly," William said, "that when you cry, the tears run down the back of your head. You have to sneak up to the mirror in case it runs away in fright." And so on.

Emma stood firm.

By now, William was completely fed up with the situation. Still clutching the case, he pushed past his sister and ran downstairs.

He just wanted to be alone to think, but his mother caught him in the hall. "William," she said, "make yourself of

29

some use. Chop some wood before breakfast."

William sighed. "Yes, Mama."

"Request time," said the case. The temptation was just too much. William pressed the button, though rather hesitantly. The case opened.

"I wish we had a winter's supply of wood. OK?"

"Not 'arf guv'nor; it's done," the case replied, very self-satisfied.

"I'll bring some wood in straight away, Mama." William went briskly outside. The snow was settling thickly on the ground, covering the churned-up lawn and whitewashing part of the broken summerhouse. William could hear his father complaining to himself that he would never be able to afford to repair the summer house and lay a new lawn. Despite this, William felt very relieved to see that in the woodshed, by the tall bare sycamore, was a large pile of ready-cut logs.

"Well, at least that wish turned out alright." As William gathered up an armful of the wood, the case hummed a curious tune to itself.

William returned with his load, rather proudly and commenced laying the fire with it. Whilst he was doing this, Mr. Harris ran in flustered, puffing like an asthmatic steam-train.

"Mrs. Whipper-Snapper mam, sum boonder's cut down all th' prize cherry trees!"

"Oh no," William muttered under his breath, staring agape at the fire. When he stood up, he saw both his mother and Mr. Harris staring suspiciously at him and the wood he had brought in.

"William...." his mother began, hardly able to contain her mounting fury.

"Mother, honestly, I...I can explain."

"Well?" his mother asked impatiently.

"Well?" Emma asked as she came in.

"It was Vizit," the case said, thinking a bad excuse better than none.

"Go to your room at once," his mother said furiously. "Your father's just gone to surgery, but I'll tell him about this when he returns. This is your last prank."

William felt defeated. Dejectedly, he went up to his room.

"Right," he said opening the case, "I wish I had never wished that last wish." There was an undertone of bitterness in his voice.

"'Fraid I can't help you old chap," the case said, coldly closing.

"Why not, for goodness sake?" William asked in an exasperated voice.

"I'm a 1.B. Prize. I don't wish to extinguish all hope, but I only grant requests, dumbo. My gyrating Domwangler won't allow me to ungrant them any longer. It's negative and Prizes are positive."

'Anymore Prizes like you and I'm done for,' thought William. "Look, please. I'm in trouble," he pleaded.

"One can't be too careful these days. Sorry."

"What are you doing?" Emma walked in.

William felt completely in the doldrums. He pressed the button and the case opened.

"I wish I had never found you," he said into the purple glow.

And he meant it.

"What are you doing?" Emma walked in.
William felt completely in the doldrums.
He pressed the button and the case opened.
"I wish I had never found you," he
said into the purple glow. And he meant it.

5

A Spirited Conversation

"'Fraid not. Try again," the case said curtly. "You cannot wish me away, snotty; negative you see. I will not be buried or hidden again. Once given, I am yours for good." It closed.

"Or bad." William felt deeply depressed by it all.

"Wh...what is it?" Emma said amazed.

"A nuisance," William said on his beam-end.

"You're as funny as a toothache," snapped the case.

"P....please Billy; I thought you were just playing tricks on me earlier. I didn't know you had, had...please, what is it?"

Emma seemed genuinely interested and so despite interruptions from the case, William felt relieved to explain how he had found it and the trouble it had caused.

"That's your opinion, buffo," the case kept saying crossly.

But for once Emma tended to believe her brother; possibly because she could think of no other explanation for a talking silver case!

"If only there was some way I could give it back and then everything would be all right. It's nothing but trouble," William said. "If only..."

"Pah!" the case interrupted. "If ifs and ands were pots and pans, where would be the Tinker? Once given, I am yours until you have a first-born child of your own, or until you snuff it!"

"Oh crimney, isn't there any other way at all?"

"Well really, I don't know why you want to get rid of me. After all, I can be of great benefit."

"I knew it. There is another way isn't there?" William suddenly brightened, seeing new hope in the case's evasiveness.

"Oh, very cunning," muttered the case begrudgingly. "Yes, turnip-head, I could be returned to the Prize-Maker. Though this would be a definite 'no-no' in my books."

Emma, stunned into silence by it all, listened intently.

"The Prize-Maker. Of course!" William exclaimed. "Where does he live, again?"

"Theomodor," the case muttered resentfully.

"Well then," William pressed the button. "I wish you back to the Prize-Maker in Theomodor."

"No, you don't!" The case showed a sense of obstinate triumph.

"You're just being deliberately difficult." William shut the case with an angry 'snap.'

"Temper, temper. No stomach was ever upset by someone swallowing an evil mood. How can you expect flowers to bloom in your heart when you have a fire in your soul?"

"Oh, for goodness sake!" William put his hand to his head in exasperation. He was discovering that a thing easily won is often the most difficult to lose.

"Don't be a grumpy bear," said the case. "Only the First-Given can return the 1.B. Prize."

"Well, who might that be?" William asked, vaguely hopeful once more.

"Oh, I've forgotten. My Droopsifier isn't quite what it was you know. If you'd been buried for so many years, your memory might start playing up as well."

Suddenly, in walked one very cross Whipper-Snapper –

34

their father. William hurriedly pushed the case under his bedclothes.

"Now boy, what is all this about my cherry trees? Whatever possessed you to chop them down?" He peered furious-eyed at William.

"But Papa, I didn't."

"It was Vizit," the case said.

"Who said that?" Dr. Whipper-Snapper glowered.

"I....I did," Emma said, surprising herself by defending her brother. Dr. Whipper-Snapper grew so angry at this that, although it was only ten in the morning, he said that they should go to bed immediately and that all they would have to eat for the remainder of the day would be bread and milk.

Leaving William, he escorted Emma to her room; his nostrils flaring like two blunderbusses about to go off.

When he heard his father's footsteps recede down the stairs, William took out the case. Emma also must have been listening to her father's going, for she crept back as soon as she knew he was safely in the hall.

"What are we going to do now, Billy?"

"Well, I hadn't thought of 'we' doing anything, Emms. But since we've called a truce, let's see how we get along." He opened the case, "Alright, I wish to speak with the one who owned you before me."

"No way, buffo! You will have to be more specific than that if you want results or you will make as much progress cutting through the problem as using a handleless sword with no blade."

"What's he talking about, Billy?" Emma was confused. William knew how she felt.

"Cutting remark," the case muttered unnecessarily.

"Emms, yesterday I was reading a book from Papa's study that, in a way, has to do with the case. The book is a type of family history, going way back many, many years to Tudor times, Henry VIII, etc. I think that this may tell us who

35

the First-Given was; or at least who had the case before it found it. It's over there, pass it to me would you."

"Get it yourself," snapped the case.

"Yes," Emma agreed.

William knew that the case was trying to stir things again. With a shrug of his shoulders, he went over and opened the book. He flicked through the pages to an earmarked section near the beginning.

"It doesn't say much, but let's see. Yes, here, it's from the parish records. 'Benjamin Whippsnappin, being Lord of Prize Hall.' Now that's a coincidence. '*Prize Hall!*' Well, that could be because of the case is a 'prize.' Benjamin was born in 1538 and died in 1585. That would be enough time for an oak tree to grow over the case that Benjamin buried for some reason before I found it." William felt pretty pleased with his *Sherlock Holmes* deduction talents!

"I must admit I do recall someone naming something after me long ago. In gratitude," the case said pointedly.

William took hold of the case. "Well, I wish to speak with Benjamin Whippsnappin now, if you please."

"You've got a ghost of a chance," the case said dryly.

There was a gush of wind and everything went suddenly rather cold and dark. A strong smell of lavender and cloves filled the room. Then, there was what could only be described as a moan.

"I'm frightened, Billy." Emma tried to stop herself shaking by grabbing hold of her brother's arm.

As quickly as a wave breaks upon a shore, the room grew lighter and the moaning grew quieter.

Both William and Emma were quite speechless. What started as a moan turned into a luminously red shape fell through one wall of William's bedroom and landed, with what would have been a loud thud if it hadn't been silent, flat on the floor.

"Wh.....what is it?" William asked the case uneasily.

"Your request, I presume, buzfuz. Who did you expect, Father Christmas?"

The shape rose up and began forming into a figure of some description. It had some difficultly standing on what were rapidly becoming its two legs. Shaking uncontrollably, the figure suddenly landed flat on its back.

Very unsteadily, it rose up once more and, though at first semi-transparent, increasingly became solid. It kept glowing red, like a beacon. The room was now completely drenched in the overpowering odour of lavender and cloves.

"....It's a ghost!" William gasped.

"What do you want, a medal?" the case asked as sarcastically as possible. "I presume it's the spirit of my previous owner, buffo. I've made it easy for you by bringing him to you. Don't bother thanking me though. I wouldn't want you to feel indebted."

"Don't you know?"

"I'm a 1.B. Prize, It is not..."

"Alright, alright," William cut the case off quickly.

"Your galumphing rudeness is as epic as ever," it snapped.

The shimmering figure managed to stand fairly firmly at last. It seemed to be a middle-aged man, dressed in what William presumed to be an Elizabethan costume. Although the red luminosity of the whole obscured much of the detail.

"Where have I been summoned?" the figure asked in a hollow, quivering voice. Its face turned an iridescent scarlet.

"You're at Callerton House," William said, summoning courage from confusion.

"Who is it that hath called me thus from yon Great Beyond? Who art thou?"

"I," William cleared his throat uneasily, "I am William Norton Whipper-Snapper. This is my sister, Emma."

"And I'm a 1.B. Prize," said the case pompously.

The ghost gave out a shriek. Flashing green sparks, it

turned and attempted to walk through the wall. However, for some reason best known to itself, it only succeeded in banging its nose, which promptly turned into a small pillar of orange fire.

"Gadzooks!" it yelled, turning back, and fanning the flame with a bright red hand. "Not thou, omen of downfall and doom. Bane of hope. Destroyer of calm." It pointed a quivering mauve finger at the case.

"He obviously recognizes you," William said, feeling a small victory come his way.

"Oh, jubjub and boojums," said the case indignantly.

"Thou took my ease from me when I walked this earth and now thou wilt not leave me to my eternal rest. Why hast thou summoned me so unkindly as thus?"

"You did own the case then?" William asked eagerly.

"Alack and alas, yon accursed thing was mine. But no more, no more. Pray let me return."

The ghost suddenly floated up to the ceiling, which he attempted to fade through. Instead, his glowing head hit it with a painful smack and he bounced giddily back down, scarlet hands clutching his head, which was flattened like a dinner plate.

"We don't want to cause you any trouble, you can go soon," William reassured the ghost. "But you see, I want to return this 'Prize' to its maker. To do this I must find the First-Giver. Was it you?"

"To return it is wise, is fruitful," the ghost said, its head returning to its proper shape like a pop-up top hat. "But alas, I am not the one you seek. I found yon cursed object wrapped in ancient cloth, locked in an ancient lead box in the wine cellar of Prize Hall. It was beneath a slab that had loosened. My hall would still rise, where this house stands, if not for yon downfall box. Everything went awry when I 'wished to be rich!' Yon case replied, 'It is done! What is your second wish, Rich?' That box 'twas as useful as a fork in sugar."

"Would you mind keeping your opinions to yourself," the case snapped resentfully.

Despite popular myths, the ghost was far more frightened than frightening. William realized that he could not return the case to him.

"Who owned the case before you, do you know?" he asked.

Emma had stopped shaking long ago and was listening intently. She thought it all really most interesting.

"I know not," the ghost turned a curious reddy-blue color, "though in the box of lead with yon bizarre trinket ….."

"Well la-de-da!"

"….was some inscribed manuscript. Though this was so long ago that I cannot recall the matter of it."

"Oh dear," William sighed, by now completely accustomed to the friendly ghost.

"Pray young master," the ghost said earnestly in pastel blue and stretching himself to the height of the bedroom, "pray let me return away from the devil box, to the place where light falls from infinitely high and darkness rises from immeasurable depths."

"Pah! Fine words butter no parsnips," snapped the case.

"Shush!" William ordered. "I'm trying to think." He had to locate that manuscript.

"Well, I suppose new experiences are good for everyone," the case commented.

"So," William decided, "I suppose I shall have to see the lead box and manuscript for myself. I will have to return to 1580 and find Benjamin and the manuscript he speaks of." He opened the case. "Then perhaps I shall find out who the first owner was." The purple glow from the case shone in his face. "I wish to see the manuscript that the ghost found with you."

"Hang onto your hat, buffo," the case said. "I'll take you there and you can see the manuscript."

"What of me?" the ghost pleaded.

"Emma, you stay here," William urged, ignoring the spirit.

But before she could protest, she found herself somewhere completely different.

"Where have I been summoned?" the ghostly figure asked in a hollow, quivering voice.

6

Much Ado About Something

"Prize Hall," William whispered to himself. "Benjamin Whippsnappin's home."

"Is it, Billy?"

William turned to see his sister at his side. "You're here too, Emms? So, the case slipped up again." William however was really quite happy that his sister had come along.

"A real grouse aren't you," the case sneered.

The room the children found themselves in smelt strongly of freshly baked bread, lavender, and cloves. It was what you might call a medium-sized room. All its walls were paneled in dark oak and had acorn designs on the edge of each panel. Large, elaborately colorful floral tapestries hung on two of the walls. Opposite them, in a carved stone fireplace, a large log fire was burning in a big iron basket. The floor was red-tiled, with a covering of lavender that had been scattered liberally all around. There was a sturdy carved oak table and chair just in front of the children.

"Where's the ghost?" Emma asked her brother.

"Somewhere else than here I presume, ink-eyes!" the case snapped testily and promptly disappeared.

"Oh dear, now what is it up to?" William gazed around to see where the case could have gotten to. "You can't leave us here," he added earnestly.

"Mean, spiteful thing," Emma complained.

"Shush," William urged. "I can hear voices and footsteps coming closer outside. Quickly Emma; let's hide before we're seen."

They turned and slid behind a large upright tapestry screen that was to the right of the high-backed oak chair.

"Billy," Emma whispered, "you don't really think I'm ugly, do you?" She was serious. William gave a quiet laugh.

"About as ugly as cherry blossoms," he said. She held his hand.

The heavily carved door opened slowly and in strode Benjamin Whippsnappin looking very, very much alive. Without his ethereal glow, he seemed almost a stranger sight. He was quite tall and head, the top which was bald, was adorned by a circle of curly chestnut hair that appeared to be rather matted and covered with whitey-mauve power. His eyes were like two large gob-stoppers, sticking out in a stare. Around his large red lips, he sported a neatly trimmed moustache and a short-pointed beard outlined his cleft chin. But really, his whole face seemed simply a foil for a cartoonishly large beaked nose, which looked as sticky as an ash bud. Ash tree buds.

But it was what he was wearing that made Emma giggle. Round his neck, he was sporting an absurdly large, white cambric ruff. His tight-fitting tunic and red doublet, quilted and padded so that his chest stuck out like a cocky pigeon's, was covered with fine yellow embroidery, and was slashed to reveal a rich purple lining beneath. He also proudly wore padded red breeches made of some clove-scented velvet. These were so enormous that it seemed as though it must be extremely difficult for him to sit down.

But it was what he was carrying that interested William; a rather large and crudely made lead box. He placed it on the table. He started humming a tune to himself that William recognized as *Greensleeves*. He went over the door, opened it,

42

and called out loudly, "Ned, bring a cup of posset and an amber porringer of March pane and violet comfits."

He shut the door and went over to the box. He tapped it. He attempted to open it, but it was either stuck or locked.

"'S' blood. 'tis a fact this box is full of willfulness!" He sighed.

The door opened. A servant rushed in wearing black trousers that were ridiculously tight and a red and white chequered tunic. He was carrying a silver tray, with a large pewter mug and a plate of sugar flowers and marzipan triangles decorated with roasted almond and pistachio nuts.

"Umm, they look quite nice," Emma whispered to herself.

After the servant had left, Benjamin took a March pane and drank from his mug, all the time contemplating the lead box.

Taking a stiletto from a velvet-covered sheath hanging from his belt, he proceeded to work the point in deeper and deeper. In due course, the box opened.

"A veritable marvel," he cried inordinately pleased with himself. Carefully he took out the silver case.

"What's it doing there?" Emma whispered to her brother.

"Well," William considered, "I suppose even the case can't be in two places at once." He fell silent as Benjamin took out a small yellow parchment scroll. He unrolled it. William had seen something like this before.

"'Tis a most crude and uneven Latin script," Benjamin said to himself, studying it carefully. "But I think I shall find its cipher. Yes - 'Beware the Talisman of Downfall. Wish no wish. Edras Whippsnapson.'"

Still hidden behind the screen, William took a pencil and paper from his pocket to write down the name Edras Whippsnapson and other notes before he would certainly forget.

Benjamin scratched his head, then rubbed his pointed beard.

"No matter. Mere heathen superstition. This must be but an ordinary box," he decided.

"I'm no ordinary box, buffo," the case announced. "I'm a 1.B. Prize and I would take it kindly if you would treat me with proper regard."

"Y'gads," Benjamin cried, dropping the case. "What hocus-pocus is this?"

"Careful, clumsy," it complained. "Just open me and make any wish you desire."

William saw Benjamin's face light up. He decided to make a move, when suddenly the door opened and in sauntered a large woman. She was wearing a ruff even more enormous than Benjamin's as well as a purple stomacher (a tunic ribbed with whalebones) that gave her an immaculately flat chest and tiny waist, from which billowed a huge purple and red, farthingale skirt. The total effect was to make her look something like a red wine glass turned topsy-turvy.

"What is it, my crystal comfit?" Benjamin held the silver case behind his back.

"Still eating, husband?" The woman had a sandpaper voice. "You broke fast, but one hour since, with baked bread, butter, fresh honey, and a large cold ham."

"Yes, my jeweled haunch of venison." Benjamin tried not to sound too agitated.

"Well my lord, do not forget that we are going to the Globe at Southwark to see the new work by the playsmith, young Master Shakespeare."

"Much Ado About Nothing," said the case.

"Pardon?" The woman eyed her husband.

"Oh.....oh the name of the play, my sweet roast gosling," Benjamin said hurriedly.

"Well, my lord, prepare thyself. We leave within this hour. It is a long journey to Southwark by coach and whirlicote."

"Yes, my precious steamed almond pudding," Benjamin gestured subserviently.

She left without a word.

"At last!" William whispered.

"What manner of thing art thou?" Benjamin asked, staring at the case.

Before an answer was forthcoming, William and Emma revealed themselves from behind the tapestry screen.

"Hallo, Benjamin," Emma said.

"Y'gads!" He picked up his stiletto from the table and pointed it threateningly at the children.

"There's no need for that Benjamin," William reassured.

"Thy strange attire. Art thou two changelings – guardians of yon silver box?"

"He doesn't know us at all," Emma said.

"Course not, messy-mouth," the case said in a know-it-all voice. "He will not meet you for over three hundred years; when he comes back as your friendly ghost you summoned to see; so kindly delivered by yours truly!"

"There's no need to be so personal," Emma retorted.

"What devilry is this?" Benjamin gasped, bewildered.

"Explain it to him, case," William said.

"Shan't! Although it's true that I am your Prize in your time, here I am this good fellow's and can only grant his instructions. Besides, buffo, I don't want to! You wished to come here, so you explain."

"Speak, changelings!" Benjamin's eyes were almost popping out of their sockets. "Speak! What manner of beings art thou?" He fingered his blade. "Ned, Jack," he yelled. "Jack, Ned."

"No! Wait!" William begged.

The door suddenly flew open and two servants rushed in.

"Hold these two fast," Benjamin said excitedly. The two

45

men seized hold of the children.

"Oh, crimney!" William struggled.

"Let go of us, Emma screamed.

"Your strange attire and jiggery-pokery fool me not. Thou art spies of her Majesty. Speak!" Benjamin glared at them.

William had to think quickly, the mood had turned decidedly nasty.

"No, my Lord," William stressed.

"What then? Wert thou of Bothwell's part? Loyal to the Queen of Scots?"

"No," said Emma.

"Yes." William gave his sister a sharp kick.

"Ow!"

"Liars!" Benjamin boomed. "Thou knowest of my part in the conspiracy to set free the Queen of Scots from the clutches of that Protestant autocrat, Elizabeth."

"No. No. Honestly, we just came to….."

"Silence!" Benjamin commanded. "Take them to the cellars. There is much at stake this day."

"Please," William pleaded, "you must understand. We're not part of anything to get you into trouble. I promise. We're….friends."

"I'd save your breath if I were you, sonny," the case said casually. "He won't believe anything you say. Why should he? Your story is a little far-fetched you must admit!"

"B…..but it's true!" William protested.

"Ah, but truth must often be seen to be true, or it might just as well be a lie!" the case explained.

"This is mine." Benjamin grabbed hold of the case. "I shall find much use for you case if you can perform all that you say."

William and Emma were dragged out of the room into the Long Hall, which was panelled in oak and had wall hangings as well as pictures painted on wood. The ceiling was decorated with plaster patterns of flowers and birds. But, of course, the children were too preoccupied to notice these things!

"Case! For goodness sake help us," William urged.

"Silence!" Benjamin ordered.

"See, you need me now; pathetic isn't it, eh?" the case said. "Well, cadger, if I may suggest, that in this situation, if you wish that you were back in your own time, I might very well comply."

"Be silent, box!" Benjamin said.

"Rudeness gets you nowhere, except disliked," the case retorted.

Then William collapsed.

"Billy!" cried Emma. "Please, something's happened to my brother. He's not well."

Benjamin went up to William's groaning figure, still held up by Ned.

"I'm not a heartless man," Benjamin said. "Release him. Then when he is revived, I shall dispatch him for good."

Ned released the stricken boy. Instead of slumping to the ground, William immediately jumped at Benjamin. He grabbed hold of the case. Then, whirling around, William gave Jack a resounding kick on the shin. Jack released Emma with a yell.

"Quickly Emms, run." William took hold of his sister's hand. They ran up the length of the hall. Benjamin and the two servants joined in pursuit, with knives drawn. The two children sped along, aiming to escape through the door at the other end.

Just as they were in touching range, the door sprang open, knocking both children flat on their backs. Above them, in billowing skirts, was the Mistress of the Hall with two maidservants.

Desperately, William pressed the case open. "I wish that Emms and I were back in our own time and place," he panted.

Immediately, the case disappeared. It returned to Benjamin's hand. He halted and stood looking menacingly down at the children. "Forsooth, thou shalt tell of nothing again."

"They are spies?" his wife asked. "Then we must dispatch them now."

"Yes, my sweet pickled starling in mint aspic."

Knives seem to close in on the children from all sides. They clutched onto each other; but when they blinked away their tears of fear, they were back in Callerton House. Through William's bedroom window, they could see that it was getting dark outside. It had taken longer than expected.

"Well, lantern jaws, was it worth it?" the case said half-mockingly.

"Y...yes," William said slightly bemused. Then he pulled something out of his pocket. It was the note he tucked away. "Look Emms. I wrote down the name – Edras Whippsnapson."

"Where the deuce have you two been?" said an angry voice. Their father was standing at the door. "Your mother came up and couldn't find hide nor hair of you. It's unlike you Emma to be so badly behaved. Well, I'm going to have to think of your punishment as both of you have disobeyed my orders. But it's getting late, so both of you get to bed at once. We will talk more of this in the morning."

Dr. Whipper-Snapper was furious. He was a man without a sense of humor at the best of times; this was the worst. Without saying another word, each child was marched into bed.

"Still want to persist with this absurd plan of returning me?" asked the case, as he lay beside the boy in bed.

"Of course!" replied the boy, "and next time, don't leave like you did!"

"That's not up to me," the case said abruptly. "Anyway, I never really left, so there! If you must go foolishly on, I would suggest next time you wish to be dressed in the attire of the time. I shall also alter your language so that everyone speaks in terms you understand, and vice versa. Don't you think that is considerate of me, buffo? See how useful I can be? Look, why don't you just keep me. It would be much wiser you know."

The case would have gone on further, but it suddenly realised that William had fallen asleep.

"Charming!" the case complained. "No manners. No manners at all!"

And it glowed a sullen purple.

"They are spies? Benjamin's wife asked.
"Then we must dispatch them at once."

The case would have gone on further, but it suddenly
realised that William had gone to sleep.
"Absolutely charming!" it complained bitterly.

7

A Ghastly Ghost and Carved Red Dragons

The Scream!

It was the scream that woke William up with such a shudder. At first, he thought it was the remnants of a nightmare. Then he heard it again. A terrible blood – curdling scream, and what was worse, William knew that it was his mother.

He jumped out of bed.

"Where are you scuttling off to?" asked the case. "Haste makes waste."

William ignored it and ran out onto the landing. He heard voices from his parent's room; the sound of his father consoling his mother. He crept closer and listened at the door.

"I tell you, dearest Henry, I saw it. I did, I surely did!"

"Now, now Emily don't distress yourself. I'm sure it was merely a night-fever."

"No! No, it wasn't Henry. I saw it. It was, *was* a ghost."

"Oh no!" William muttered to himself. "Benjamin! Can't that case do anything properly?"

"What is it, Billy?" Emma had emerged from her bedroom.

"It's that stupid ghost; he's still in the house."

"Oh goodness! And he's frightened Mama?"

"Yes, it's ghastly. As if there wasn't enough trouble without this."

They both went back to his bedroom. William felt very cross with the case. All of a sudden, there was a clatter and a crash. Benjamin's ghost, glowing red, fell out of William's cupboard. He landed flat on his face. Promptly, he rolled himself up like a train's window blind and unfurled himself in an unsteady standing position. He floated two feet above the floor and gave off occasional green sparks.

"Why didst thou not return me to yon sphere beyond," the ghost wailed.

"I don't like you!" Emma said in a surly voice.

"Yes," William agreed. "You should be ashamed of yourself threatening innocent children; wanting to lock them up in your cellar! Or worse!"

"I should save your breath if I were you," the case said knowingly. "He won't remember one iota of your visit to his time. When you vanished from Prize Hall, with my able assistance, all the people of his time forgot completely that they had ever seen you. I saw to that, sonny. All part of the service; don't bother to thank me."

"I won't," William replied rather unreasonably. "Why haven't you gotten rid of the ghost? It's frightened my mother and goodness knows what else!"

"Won't"

"Crimney, why not?"

"'Cos I can't. In life you can't hope to have convenient explanations for everything, you know, buffo. Most reasons are deep and meaningless anyway. I always say!"

"Well don't bother!" Emma retorted. "You're simply horrid, that's all!"

"Woe is me," moaned the ghost turning puce and twirling on his head. "Yon case is the box of sadness beyond time."

"Oh go chew a bluebottle!" the case snapped.

"When my darling gallon honey pot buried you, I thought that would be an end to it; alas 'twas not to be."

"Why did your wife bury the case?" William asked.

The ghost sobbed and green tears the size of ping-pong balls bounded up his cheek (for he was still topsy-turvy) and melted into mauve light, just before touching the floor.

"Alack, yon case bade me wish things, and alas I did. I wished for an extension to my Hall to make it the finest in the land, even removing a hill that rose behind it. But it drew attention to me and made people suspicious. I also wished for my cause to be realised. Then, when the Queen of Scots met her demise, I wished that I might not be discovered in my house. Oh, woe. I was taken by the Royal Yeomen; captured as I was conducting business in London. I was seeking to cover my past actions, but it was a trap set by Queen Elizabeth's men, who discovered my part in wanting to help the Scottish Queen. Yon case had not helped me at all. I was found guilty of plotting the freedom of Queen Mary. For a time I was imprisoned in the Tower of London; then…let's just say it didn't end well."

"What a jolly little tale," the case said sarcastically. "But, I have brought you back after three hundred years so you can moan to these two now. You should thank me."

The ghost sighed. "For a time I haunted the Tower. But I could never master the Haunting Profession. When I failed to get my 'Chains,' which are the signs of a successful spook, I was relegated to haunting Prize Hall. I saw my darling smoked salmon pie bury yon case and plant a tiny oak sapling over it. I thought peace would fall upon my house then, instead, my house fell down, collapsed. My family became as poor as church mice. With nowhere else to haunt, I was put out to pasture in the Great Beyond. 'Tis an uneventful, yet restful way of passing eternity."

"Well, don't blame me, spooky lad," said the case. "When it comes to humans, you spin your own yarns but where you end up is really, in fact, where you always intended to be – whether you knew it or not!"

"Benjamin, that's quite a sad story," William admitted. "Very sad, in fact."

"Oh yes, yes. It's easy to be kind to someone who means nothing to you," the case said vehemently. "I told him the foundations wouldn't stand an enormous extension to Prize Hall. Really, it's just too bad! Why must you all speak in headlines and blame everything but yourselves? Weak foundations, greedy people, careless people; that's the cause of most wrongs in your world. You people always blame anyone else for your misfortunes, never yourselves. Get all the money you want, but no one's rich enough to buy back the things he's done wrong. You don't realise that your own selfish wishes carry your mistakes with them. Think of what you wish for. I for one..."

"Alright, alright. Crimney, don't go on so," William sighed, "no one blames you for everything."

"I do," Emma said.

"And I." The ghost rolled himself into a ball and unraveled himself upright again.

"Cooo, ain't it luvly!" the case complained. "Don't know why I bother."

And William wondered why he bothered as well.

"Well anyway, we have to settle this as soon as possible," William said firmly. "I have to find out if the name I wrote down, Edras Whippsnapson, is the key to returning the case to the Prize-Maker. I have to find out if Edras Whippsnappson was the First-Given. I can't risk bringing him here; two ghosts would be just too much to cope with! Emms, you stay here and look after Benjamin."

"Yes Billy," Emma agreed. She felt too tired to argue.

William pressed open the case.

"I wish to go back to the past again; to the time of Edras Whippsnapson." He was about to add something more, but

54

the words didn't have a chance to come out. As fast as saying 'Oh!' he was standing in the open beside a rough road. William had to give the case its due – it really did make travelling back in time easy. Perhaps a little too easy!

There was a strong smell of wood smoke in the air, swirling around his nose and eyes. In the distance, William could see a line of soldiers marching up the road that wound through two hills like the ash smoke that curled ribbons into the overcast, slate-grey sky. The soldiers, as far as he could make out, were armed with shields, swords, and spears. There were also several mounted soldiers wearing chain mail and carrying lances. It was just like a picture from one of his history books come vividly to life.

Hearing someone behind him, William rapidly turned. "Crimney, Emms!" he exclaimed, astonished. "How on earth did you get here?"

"How do you think? It's that silly case's fault!"

"Hold your tongue," the case said indignantly. "I haven't hob-nobbed with 1.A. Prizes to be insulted by you, dumbo."

William took a long look at his sister. "Well, at least we're dressed for the part, Emms. I think!"

"Yes, I noticed, Billy. They're not very comfortable."

"Don't make such personal remarks," the case added.

William was wearing a dark brown woolen tunic, with a braided belt of bronze, and shoes with long leather leggings. Emma was wearing a cloth dress of forest green, over which she had a rough woolen shawl of darkish blue. The shawl was worn over one shoulder, coming down and tucked in at her belt. Her hair was plaited in Saxon fashion.

From the fast-moving line of soldiers, like a landscape of sound as a north wind blew wine-dark clouds across the sky, there came this rousing, though somewhat weary cry: "Long may Harold Godwinson hold dominion over these isles. Invaders who come laughing shall soon lose their

55

smiles."

"Should we hide, Billy?"

"No, Emms. We must ask to speak with Edras Whippsnapson. I only hope that Benjamin isn't causing any trouble back in our time. Do you know if he is, case?"

"How should I know!" it said and promptly vanished.

William shrugged his shoulders in a resigned way. The line of soldiers was drawing ever nearer. William couldn't help feeling rather apprehensive. He was just about to suggest that perhaps it would be a good idea if they were to hide when there was a loud 'neigh' at his back and a clatter of metal on metal.

Both children turned. A mounted figure was peering down at them. He was tall in the saddle, with a stern face, that although unshaven and rather dirty, retained his proudly, handsome features. He was wearing a thick brown leather tunic, beneath a long waistcoat of chain mail that appeared to be slightly rusting. Obviously, this mounted figure was a seasoned warrior. William swallowed uneasily.

The man's leather helmet, strengthened with metal bands, was slung over the top of his large shield, which bore the emblem of a Red Dragon carved on it and was strapped to the side of his mud-splattered steed. A long javelin was strapped below this, with a battle-axe. At his waist hung a large sword with a yellow bone handle and red leather thonging.

"And who may you two siblings belong to?" the man said gruffly. "Are you from some village yonder? It is a fair walk from any house and dusk is falling, so why do you wait here?"

"We're looking for Edras Whippsnapson," William said.

"Are you, young gadfly? Well then, you need look no further." The rider steadied his horse. He eyed them suspiciously.

"Come then," he urged. "I am Edras Whippsnapson,

56

Captain of Earl Edmund and faithful thane to Harold Godwinson. But who wishes to know this? What is it you want? Answer quickly; I have not time to squander on children."

"Charming!" Emma muttered under her breath.

The soldiers approached.

"We have come about the silver case," William said as clearly as he could.

Edras jumped down from his mount, chain mail and sword clanging. He took hold of the children by the scruffs of their necks.

"Let go of us," William said in a fluster. Emma tried her very best not to start crying.

"What do you know of the talking talisman?" Edras boomed. "Are you robber's children? Are you Norman spies?"

"No," Emma cried. "Why does everyone think we're spies?"

"Honestly we aren't." William sounded as sincere as he could under the circumstances. Both their feet were dangling in the air.

"We....we have one just the same," William added desperately. "We just want to tell you what we've found out about it."

"Really, we do," Emma pleaded.

Edras dropped them. "Edras Whippsnapson needs advice from no one. I have long to march and much to do before true rest. But I shall keep you awhile. Mind you, don't turn coward and think with your feet. No one can outrun my steed."

"Th....that's fine," William agreed nervously.

Like driftwood smouldering in a grate, the sun was reddening the last embers of the ash-grey day. A soldier came up to Edras.

"Captain, shall we march on to the village?" His voice

was deep and clear.

"No. Dusk is down. We have marched long this day. Strike up camp here."

The soldier nodded in salute. Going back to the line of men, he shouted some orders. The foot soldiers laid down their arms. Those on horseback dismounted.

Edras led the two children over to the other side of the rough, winding road, where the soldiers were busily setting up their overnight camp.

"Guthram, watch these two for me," Edras said to an absurdly tall, bearded soldier, wearing a large dirty-white woolen jerkin over his brown tunic. On his blond head, he sported a huge horned helmet. He was leaning on an enormously savage two-handed battle-axe.

William eyed the figure anxiously. Emma held his hand so tightly that his knuckles went white. Edras strode purposefully off.

"Do let's go home, Billy."

"I know how you feel, Emms, but it's impossible until we find out if Edras is the First-Given."

"Quiet," Guthram said, in a not-too-unkind growl that was heavily laced with a foreign accent.

There was a distinct chill in the air, though judging by the oak and ash trees around still full of leaf, it must have been late summer; probably September.

The two children watched the campfires being lit, welcoming the warm glow of burning wood.

"You want food?" Guthram asked the children.

There was some meat of an indescribable nature roasting over the flames. William and Emma settled for some rather dry, unleavened bread and water.

William watched, as two soldiers passed by carrying two long wooden poles, each with a carved red dragon on top. The men were talking of some great victory against the Vikings; how their High King, Harold Godwinson, would surely overcome the crown-threatener from across the wide water; how all the invaders would end defeated and in thralldom.

"What does all this mean, Billy?"

"I can only make out some of it, Emms; but it doesn't matter, I think that we shall soon know." William nodded to the right.

Out of the soldier's seated ranks, the dark figure of Edras Whippsnapson, flickering in the campfire light, strode towards them.

By the welcoming, warming glow of the camp fire, William and Emma settled for some rather dry, unleavened bread.

An impressive, mounted figure was peering down at them.

Chapter 8

A Norman Conquest

"You two, come with me."

The children followed Edras to a roughly erected tent, made from four tied poles and animal skins stretched over as a cover.

"Inside!" he, rather abruptly, directed the children as he held up a rough-edged skin flap, eyeing them suspiciously.

The tent within was dark and musky, though there was some light, for a small fire had been lit and there was a hole in the skin above the fire to allow the smoke out.

"Now tell me, what is it that you know of the talking talisman?" He held up the silver case.

"Hallo, we've got to stop meeting like this!" it remarked.

"What spirit gives it voice?" Edras asked inquisitively, still bemused by its vocal ability.

"You tell 'em, kid," the case said.

"Well," William began somewhat hesitantly, "well, we know that this case is a .... 'prize' of some sort."

"1.B. Prize, hotch-potch."

"Be silent," Edras commanded.

The case grunted disapprovingly.

"And that it grants wishes," William added.

"That it does," Edras agreed, sitting on the ground,

"though back-handed perhaps." He directed the children to also sit; which they promptly did. His mood seemed to have softened. He began speaking, almost as if to himself.

"Before I even considered asking that case for help, we had a stirring victory at the great bridge at Stamford. It was an awesome trial of strength and our forces won the day." The glint in his deep-browned eyes showed the fervour of the recollection. "We mustered in the North way beyond Wessex and Mercia. We witnessed the approach of three hundred or more Norse longships rowing up the wide Humber, each bristling with their weapons like bloodthirsty Vikings. Ha!" He laughed, stroking the hilt of his sword. "My good blade, Dragonsbite, flashed into Norse helms, and made me proud. The Viking, Harald Hardrada, and the accursed traitor, Tostig, were both destined to feel our righteous wrath."

He paused and eyed the children as if to check they were both listening. They remained silent.

"Before the battle," Edras continued, "twenty armoured knights rode forward from our English line; one was my Lord Edmund, the leader of our knights. He called to our enemy, Tostig, saying that his brother Harold Godwinson, the King of England, offered him the Earldom of Northumbria if he would make peace.

"Ha! And what else?" Tostig asked haughtily. "What does my *fine* brother offer my noble ally Harald Hardrada?"

"'To the Viking invader, Harald Hardrada, our King offers his height, seven feet, of English ground,' was the proud Lord Edmund's reply; emphasizing the Viking's impending doom. Lord Edmund went to his other knights and they rode back to our line. The enemy refused the gracious offers.

"Then, the battle was joined. It was hard and fierce. The English charged the Viking shield wall and were repulsed. But, with another charge, backed by English bowmen, the Viking shield wall broke and we charged for the rout and won a legendary victory.

"Yet, as they fell around him, the giant Viking Harald Hardrada seemed to go berserk. He charged madly forward, his men rallied behind him with a new spirit filling their breasts. We fell back in confusion at the sudden resurgence, but soon regained our resolve and charged back. The fight was short-lived and Harald Hardrada fell to win his seven-foot of English soil. Aye, the Vikings didn't know what hit them."

"Poetic justice," the case remarked.

Edras drew a heavy sigh. A sorrowful look crept into his rugged, battle-used features. "Justice, hah! Perhaps! At one time, when Harald Hardrada and Tostig, seemed to be gaining strength, I thought the confusion on our side was too much and this talisman begged a wish. So, I wished for victory. Oh, sure enough, only twenty-four longships fled away, carrying their wounded back to the accursed Norse Lands and Tostig and Harald were no more. But my friend and comrade, Lord Edmund, fell also. So, mayhap, my wish was granted backhanded. I never held with magic before, 'tis a trickery that can turn on you like a devil hound. Only hard fighting and skill can endure to achieve triumph. Not this...this talisman."

"Some folks make you feel at home and others make you wish you were. A little gratitude never went amiss, you know!" said the case bitterly. "It is convenient to have a scapegoat. Failure in any form makes you feel better if you can blame someone else. But the truth is that you did win and Edmund would probably have fallen anyway! Glory is expensive."

"Still your demon's tongue," Edras threatened.

The case sighed knowingly.

Edras fixed the children with a steely stare.

"What Magician or Wizard fashioned this talisman?" he asked.

63

"Well, that's the whole point. You see, we don't know," William said, adding with anticipation, "Where did you find it?"

"Stop referring to me as 'it,' saucer-eyes," the case snapped.

Edras snorted, "So young one, I am to answer your questions; you have no answer to mine. Well, so be it. Perhaps if I tell you, you will tell me more, eh?"

"Yes, yes of course."

"Well, the talisman was in the Long Barrow burial tomb of a great chieftain of this area."

"Oh," William sighed, attempting to hide his disappointment; realising Edras was not the First-Given.

"Bad luck," said the case. "Don't trust gravity – it always lets you down."

"Oh, shut up you!" Emma retorted. "You're giving me a toothache."

"Oh, MY! I forgot the world revolves around you!" sneered the case. "My apologies, how silly of me. Do you know your face makes onions cry?"

"Wh...what do you know of this great chieftain?" William asked intensely. "Do you know his name and the time in which he lived?"

"His tomb dates from the early ages of the Druid Overlords. As for his name, the only clue to it is an inscription on a large bronze pin that is in my grandmother's keeping. All I recall of this is 'Telmar Rogg Arob Naq.'" Edras paused. William could tell that he had a tale to relate.

"I grew up in a village beside that Long Barrow. My grandmother educated me in the skills of reading and writing. She told me that I must guard the treasures within the tomb with my life, for this chieftain was our distant ancestor. I was going to become a priest, believe it or nay, but then one night I found the tomb desecrated. I saw one of the robbers, but could not catch him then; but I followed in pursuit, his face firmly in my thoughts. For two years I tracked him. At last, helped by a voice in my head, which I now know to be the talisman's, I found him in Great Winchester, capital of trade, thieving with his brother as was his only occupation. He had sold or bartered most of the things he had stolen, except this talisman. I dispatched him for his trouble, though his brother escaped my sword. The talisman then spoke to me and when I took it back to the village, I thought it an omen of good fortune. It is not."

"Let's not get silly about this," the case reprimanded.

"Silence!" Edras boomed. "Doubts besiege me now," he continued. "News has come from the other side of London, that William the Bastard has landed with seven hundred ships, a hundred men in each, at Pevensey Bay on the coast of Sussex. We must march full three hundred leagues from North to South of King Harold Godwinson's realm. Although much of our army, especially the main body of our archers, remain in the North, we go to London. I know steel will sing our victory. I want no part of this magic."

"Oh, dear," William muttered, "1066, the Battle of Hastings, and all that!" William remembered his lessons and how 1066 is one of the very most important dates in English History. It changed everything.

"Eh!" said Edras. "What do you know of Hastings? What battle do you speak of? Who are you?" Edras got up, very agitated. "Who are you?"

"Look," William began quickly, "if you can take us to your village so that we can see the inscription on the pin, I'm sure we can do something about the case."

"But you can't change the course of history, duncaid!" the case said mockingly.

"Pah, children!" Edras snorted. "Why should I, who have seen so much deceit, trust two strange children?" He lowered his voice. "Yet, I shall. I shall. Come, we must hurry. 'Tis a fair night ride from here. My wife and child now live with my grandmother; we must come and go without disturbing them."

The three went outside. The campfires were either smouldering out or being renewed. Guthram was still standing guard outside the tent.

"Guthram, bring two horses," Edras commanded. With a nod, the tall Dane went off into the darkness and returned a few moments later with two mounts. William was given a horse. Emma, despite her protests that she was quite capable of riding on her own, had to ride with Edras.

The campfires grew smaller, like burning flowers closing up, as they rode into the night. Over a hill they went, faster and faster. William felt fresh and excited as the wind whistled invisibly through his hair. Thus, they road for over three hours at a steady space.

Down a long lonesome road, bordered on both sides by a black hemlock hedge they sped and into a valley. Suddenly, Edras drew his horse to a halt. Immediately, William's horse did likewise. Their mounts clumped their hooves.

"There," Edras pointed, "there in the distance; you see the outline of that large, flat-topped hill and the houses at its foot?"

"Yes," William said. "Is that your village?"

Edras threw back his head joyfully, "Yes," he said and spurred his horse up on its hind legs. Side by side they rode full pace to their destination.

Soon they found themselves amidst wooden, thatched buildings. William trotted after Edras to a building nearest the hill.

"Here," the warrior said. They dismounted.

"Such a bumpy ride!" Emma complained to herself.

"Wait here. We must not disturb my family. I'll take the pin without waking them. I have no time to waste on sad farewells." Edras went inside the house.

The children waited outside. William couldn't help

feeling that they were being watched by a pair of very unfriendly eyes. He was beginning to grow rather worried when Edras finally emerged. They all moved away from the house.

"Here." Edras handed William a large bronze pin set with blue and amber beads. William looked at it closely; he could make neither head nor tail of most of the inscription. Only one section of it appeared understandable in the flickering lights of Edras's torch.

"Dar Zar Telmar Rogg – Arob Naq. Arob Naq!" William pondered. "Arob Naq. Would that be a name, case?"

"Well it's not a description!" the case said bluntly, adding, "why not take a leisurely wander to the tomb, there's more evidence there to be found. Trust me."

"I grow weary of this," Edras sighed. "There is nothing at the tomb but a carving of symbols."

"Symbols? Edras, please may we see them? It might help." William asked earnestly.

"So be it, but then let that be an end to it."

Leaving the horses tethered, Edras led the children to the other side of the hill. There they came to a long mound.

"Here," he said. The children looked closer. It had been disturbed. There were some pieces of cloth that looked like the ancient remains of a cloak and tunic. There was also a fairly large round stone. William knelt down. On it was a carving of a great bird with a frog-like creature riding it. Further along was a figure of a giant handing something to a much smaller figure. Beside this figure were two other figures, one seemingly a girl. Above their heads was something that resembled a shooting star.

"Very interesting," William mused. "I suppose what the giant is handing to this figure could be the case."

"Could indeed, fudge-face," said the case testily. "It's impossible to underestimate you."

"So..." Edras began. He didn't have time to continue.

Hearing a rustling sound from a hedge nearby, he turned and saw two figures emerge from the shadows.

"Who is it?" William turned anxiously. Emma clung to his arm.

"'Tis I," one of the figures said in a vicious voice. "I, Wiglaf, brother of your enemy, Olaf, whom you, Edras Whippsnapson, defeated. I have long awaited your return, away from the protection of your soldiers."

"And I am Arne, the accomplice," said the accomplice. "People are so afraid of me that even their eyebrows run away!"

"Accursed Danes," Edras said drawing his sword, Dragonsbite. Wiglaf and his accomplice, both with swords drawn, lunged at him. Edras parried both their blades. Emma cringed as metal crashed against metal. Wiglaf's blade hit Edras's, but clattered off the chain mail without harming him.

With a swerving motion, Edras caught Arne's sword and sent it flying upwards out of his hand. Knowing what was good for him, the accomplice sped off like a spider off a hot plate. "I'm not retreating – I'm simply advancing in the other direction," Arne shouted as he disappeared from sight.

"Now, 'tis just you and I," Edras growled, driving his sword into the curving crash of Wiglaf's blade. As Edras jumped forward at his attacker, the case fell from his tunic onto the floor.

"It was getting rather uncomfortable in there," the case said. "Well, you've got your name, aren't you going to wish yourself back, buffo?"

"What about Edras?" Emma asked anxiously, watching the two men locked in mortal combat. Wiglaf had taken out his knife and was attempting to plunge it into Edras's unprotected side. Edras grasped his hand. Sword locked against sword as they commenced a desperate wrestle for victory.

There was a loud cry as Wiglaf grabbed Edras, who

managed to forcefully bring the hilt of his sword up, smacking Wiglag's hand. Wiglaf gave way. He threw a knife at Edras, which bounced harmlessly off his chain mail. Then he ran off, cursing into the night: "I will be back. I will never forget this!"

"There, does that answer your question?" the case said. William hurriedly picked it up, opened it, and wished to return.

"Wait," Edras called, "wait, who are you? Where do you come from?"

"You would never believe us. Goodbye," said William.

"Goodbye," Emma added. But Edras never heard the farewell; before she had reached 'bye,' the children were back in William's bedroom. Both were dressed once more in normal clothing.

It was daylight. It had started snowing yet again. William and Emma sat on the bed, both exhausted by their travel.

"Poor Edras," Emma said at last.

"Yes," William agreed. "Wish I knew what happened to him."

"Why certainly," the case said, rather obligingly. "Firstly, understand that he never remembered having met you; it was as if you had never really been there. As soon as you had gone, he assumed that he had travelled to his village to see his family and pay his respects to the tomb. I remained with him, right through his return, his march to London, and his joining with the forces of King Harold Godwinson on the fateful journey to Hastings. Then, the battle – October 1066. Curious, he didn't use me for a wish, didn't even wish for victory. Silly, really!"

"Sensible, I'd call it," Emma said.

"Do stop gassing. Your mouth's so big, you could eat a banana sideways," the case retorted. "Anyway, King Harold Godwinson and his English army stood on the ridge near

Hastings as William the Bastard's and his Norman men deployed themselves. There were seven thousand soldiers on each side. The English made a shield wall that was almost impenetrable, had it been properly backed up by bowmen. I told Edras, but la-de-da, he wouldn't listen. Even so, the wall of shields beat off three fierce Norman onslaughts.

"But on 14th October, as morning lengthened, a fourth Norman attack broke the shield wall. The rout began. Without enough English arrows to beat them back, the Normans manoeuvred in for victory. It was then, out of desperation he said, that Edras wished for King Harold Godwinson's body to be protected. Well, that's the nuisance of it all. I always say be specific. Nothing touched King Godwinson's body, but that arrow hit him straight in the....well, you know the rest. Have a read about the Norman Conquest and how they took over England in your history books when you get home. And don't forget to read how the Norman's introduced castles to Britain and how they rebuilt all the major churches in stone! Fascinating stuff and nice to have experienced some of it first-hand. Certainly satisfied my Somniscope's spectrum."

"What about Edras?" Emma asked.

"I was coming to that! As soon as the English were routed, Edras escaped and returned, battle-scared, to his village. He never made a wish again. I feel he rather unjustly blamed me for the defeat. Ridiculous of course."

"Of course!" exclaimed a hollow, quivering voice. Benjamin, glowing scarlet, suddenly tumbled down through the ceiling.

"Oh, dear," William sighed, "still here then?"

"Yes, I am, because of yon box." He pointed a sizzling purple finger at the case, and his nose caught fire.

"You're using up my air," snapped the case. "Be quiet or vanish, you jingly-brained yashmak!"

"Stay here," William urged. The ghost hovered beside him, which made William feel rather uncomfortable.

70

"Anyway," the case began, "if you will allow me to continue! Edras's village took the news of the English defeat very gravely indeed. However, they treated Edras like a hero. Then, it was, that he grew foolish enough to want to get rid of yours truly."

"Foolish, Pah!" Benjamin scoffed derisively and vanished.

"Oh no, where's he gone?" Emma exclaimed.

"Oh, never mind about old dribble-bib," the case said impatiently. "As I was saying, Edras wouldn't see reason. He placed me in a lead box with the note, then took me to the burial tomb in the Long Barrow. That, by the way, is where Prize Hall was built; the tomb being directly below its wine cellar. Benjamin discovered me when he was having the cellar made larger. He certainly *loved* his wine. Anyway, as Edras was finishing the job of burying me, that grim villain, Wiglaf and two others jumped him from behind and the next thing I knew was, when I managed to loosen that slab in the cellar, I was found by that goon, Benjamin Whippsnappin."

"I like Edras." Emma said. "He had good sense and hopefully lived a long and happy life. Edras…."

"Edras schmedras!" snapped the case. "What about me, stuck for centuries in a dark, stuffy box. Poor Edras indeed!"

"Even so, it is an interesting story," William said. "Well, I suppose the next step is to go back to the time of Arob Naq. I hope to goodness he's the First-Given."

"Oh, it all seems so much bother," Emma sighed.

"Oh cha-cha-cha, it is, it is," the case stressed. "Why don't you just keep me? I can clean the house, wash the carriages, cook a fine meal; Haute Cuisine, if I say so myself."

Suddenly, there was a shattering sound of plates being broken downstairs mixed with the frantic screams of two people.

"Oh, crimney!" said William. "Here we go again."
"Yes, Edras 'shmedras' buried me. How rude!"
complained the case,
"However, if you must know, Edras sent Wiglaf
and his two thugs packing and was unharmed.
Happy now?"

9

Ghost of a Chance or Chance of a Ghost

"Mama!" Emma cried; the screaming made her feel like she had jumped into a pool of ice-cold water.

"Really, your mother has got a deplorable voice," the case commented. "It's enough to make me tarnish."

"Well, I wish you would you horrid thing," Emma retorted.

"Yes," William agreed. "Sometimes case, you're enough to make every drop of blood boil in a person's body."

"Hahaha, pickled nostrils!" snapped the case resentfully. "You're like a mountain range – hill-arious!"

But the children had left the room and were running down the stairs towards the source of the commotion.

"Where the deuce have you two been?" their father said as he emerged from his Surgery. The children were speechless. "Well, never mind now. But what was the awful screaming?" he asked.

"Mama," Emma replied excitedly.

"In the kitchen, I think," William added.

The three hurried down the stairs. William dreaded what he might see; he had come to expect just about anything and really, who could blame him?

As they entered, they saw the prostrate form of Martha.

Mrs. Whipper-Snapper, on her bended knees, was feeding her cold water from a willow-pattern cup.

"Oh, Henry," she said to her husband, "we both saw it this time."

"Saw what Emily?" asked Dr. Whipper-Snapper in a rather disconcerting voice.

"*IT*," Mrs. Whipper-Snapper said, getting up. "We both saw it. It came floating through the wall, knocked some plates off the table, and then went across into the range with a crash and flattened like a corn cake and caught fire."

"Us did see it, joost you believe madam. Fair flummoxed us it did." Martha added as she sat up.

"Hum," Dr. Whipper-Snapper contemplated. "A lot of strange things have been happening in the last few days. It's becoming intolerable! As if I didn't have enough to worry about. Well, it's all got to be sorted out; I simply won't abide in muddle." He turned to the children who, not knowing what to do, said nothing.

"Off you go. I want to talk to your mother. Keep out of trouble and keep out of my way."

The children obeyed their father immediately and went somewhat wearily back to William's bedroom.

"Well, it's obvious that we have to sort all this mess out as soon as possible," William said, holding back a yawn.

"Poor Pap is worried about the money as well as everything else."

"Perhaps he could get it from a bank," Emma said thoughtfully.

"Bank, schmank," the case said bitterly. "A bank is a place where they will lend you money, provided you can prove that you don't need it. Money is too expensive. Don't talk to me about banks."

"Actually, we weren't!" William said in a very irritated voice. "Anyway, what do you know about banks? They're for all the different people, not little silver cases."

"Oh yes, 'people,' huh you all look the same to me," retorted the case. "Now, I can tell a 1.B. Prize from a 2.C. Special any day of the century."

"I'm tired." Emma's eyes were half-closed.

"Yes, I think we ought to have a rest," William said.

"Rest!" exclaimed the case. "Oh, battered sausages. Even that bob-tailed buffoon of a ghost has more *life* than you two."

"Oh, why don't you swallow some glue and belt up," Emma said. Without waiting for an indignant reply, she walked out of William's room to her own.

William lay on his bed, ignoring the case's banter as best he could.

William realised that he would have to act soon. If he knew what Benjamin had begun to feel, he would have acted sooner. Because, you see, Benjamin was beginning to enjoy haunting the Whipper-Snapper household. He considered it a great treat to roam about in all shapes and colours, scaring people. It gave him a sense of purpose and, if he became frightening enough, he might even win his 'Chains.' Now that would be something to show the other spirits back in the Beyond!

He was even beginning to think that the case wasn't such a bad chap after all. Why, if it hadn't been for it, he might never have been called up again. All in all, it was all working out rather well.

He moaned playfully and sent Walters scampering, like a spider on a hot plate, out into the snow. It was all too much for her.

Ghosts, you understand, are like that, forever changing their minds. Well, I suppose you can't blame them; they have no bodies to change, after all!

It was William's mother calling that supper was ready that woke William. Outside, white snowflakes were set off almost luminously by the deep texture of the night. "White raisins in a black pudding," the case commented inaccurately.

William wandered out of his room to wake Emma up. He considered it curious how in the last couple of days his feelings about certain things had changed so. He now found himself actually liking his sister. He was also coming round to realise the merits of doing things for yourself, not putting the burden of achieving something on the dubious shoulders of luck, wishes, and dreams. One could say, in fact, that finding the case had, in some ways, opened his eyes.

Emma had difficulty opening hers. She still felt tired. However, as willing as a cat into water, she followed her brother down to supper.

Their father was not there. He had gone to the home his friend, Mr. Maltravers Muchbuck, the Banker, to arrange a loan to rebuild the summerhouse. However, the main topic of conversation, with their mother doing all the conversing, was the strange disappearance of Walters. She had suddenly packed her bags and left. Mrs. Whipper-Snapper had seen her running down the path at full gallop and she thought that it might be that ghost again. William and Emma couldn't help but agree.

They finished their meal and were shanghaied into putting the finishing touches to the Christmas tree.

"Hurry up, Emms," William whispered to her. "We've got something to sort out, pronto."

Within a few minutes, both children were back in William's bedroom. So, surprise, surprise was Benjamin. He was floating characteristically about three feet or so above the floor in a lying position, glowing pink, with his legs crossed. However, uncharacteristically, he did indeed appear to be inordinately pleased with himself.

"What do you suppose has come over him, Billy?"

"I dread to think!"

For no apparent reason at all, Benjamin's head was inside an enormous cube of ice.

"Ah, the fine siblings returneth," Benjamin proclaimed. The ice-cube shattered into tiny blue triangles, balls, rectangles, polygons, and cylinders that burst into a thousand multi-colored sparks as soon as they touched the ground.

"Goodness!" the children exclaimed together.

"Yes, getting rather good, isn't he?" the case said proudly. "Must admit I've given him some advice; keeping up his 'spirit' as it were."

"You've what! Oh crimney, this is getting worse and worse."

"Not worse; better," Benjamin said happily. "Yonder case and I have discussed the matter of your desire to return it. We have both arrived at a fine agreement, viz; you shouldn't."

"What my fine floating friend feels is that both he and I would like to stay here," the case emphasised.

"Indeed so," Benjamin added in a jubilant marigold glow. "A faithful friend is a strong defense and he that hath found such a one hath found a true prize, I always say."

"Well, I don't!" William said firmly. "I don't believe it." He looked at Emma. "A silver case that talks and a crazy ghost agreeing that they should stay in *our* house!"

"Very obliging of them, I'm sure!" Emma was becoming too confused to be amazed.

William picked up the case. "Emms, you really must stay behind now. I don't know how things may turn out," he said.

"No, Billy. I want to come with you. If this... this whoever he is, is the First-Given, then I want to see him."

"Alright," William smiled, admiring her pluck.

He pressed the case's purple button.

"Won't you reconsider?" urged the case. "As they say; learn to forgive others, but never yourself. I have a reputation you know."

"Well, I've never forgiven myself for finding you if

that's what you mean!" William was adamant.

"Yes, and our reputation grows with every failure," Emma added for good measure.

"That's as funny as swallowing a cart-horse!" snapped the case.

"Pah!" Benjamin added, in a deep, wailing banshee voice and shattered himself into myriads of glittering pieces of coloured gems and vanished, bit by bit.

"Up to more mischief," Emma commented as the last bit disappeared.

"No doubt," William agreed, "and the only way to stop this chaos is like this. Case, I wish to go back to the time of Arob Naq to talk with him."

"As you desire, turncoat, but you'll be very, very, very sorry. Just you mark my words." The case's tone was laden with begrudging menace.

William turned to gaze out of his window. Through the frame, he saw white petals of snow still being scattered in a cold racing wind. Suddenly, a shape began to emerge. William held his breath.

For now, the window and its frame had vanished.

10

Trouble with Jinntars
and Other Problems

No snow. Not even night any longer, but day that was still as crystal. The sky was almost golden. There was a vague smell of wildflowers and grass. It was quite warm.

William and Emma were standing in a clear expanse, covered with heather and low bushes. Beyond, around in the distance, a huge oak forest rose and stretched to shoulder some low, motionless clouds.

Not too far in front, the children could see a hill. It looked familiar somehow. Around the hill, starting from the bottom, a deep ditch had been dug and cut to an even circle, inside of which was piled earth-supporting timber ramparts. There were three such fortifications in all; the last being around the brow of the hill. On the top, was what appeared to be a collection of houses, a small village in fact.

"Goodness knows what century this is," William said.

"Don't ask me," snapped the case. "You pays your money and takes your choice, buffo. I ate a clock yesterday – it was very time-consuming!"

"Oh, I'm itching so," Emma complained.

"Yes, so am I rather," William agreed. "Crimney, case, can't you make these clothes more comfortable?"

"All this and heaven too, eh? Well, what you wear

reveals more than what you say," the case said, "so try this."

"Ugh!" Emma cried. "You horrid beast, you've covered us with dry mud!"

"It will add another layer to your skin and prevent irritation, slobber-mouth," the case replied testily. "You know it is going to be a bad day when the letters in your alphabet soup spell D-I-S-A-S-T-E-R."

"You talk nonsense! I think I'd rather itch," William said, flicking some dirt from his eye.

"Never satisfied," the case complained. "Well, I'll remove some, but leave on the rest. They all tend to be rather dirty round here, so you'll blend in like butter."

Apart from the dirt, William was wearing a sleeveless dark brown tunic that was quite course. It fell to just above his knees and was gathered at his waist to give a short, kilt-like effect. The leather belt that held it was crudely carved with what appeared to be some forms of wild animals. A short cloak, semi-circular in shape and fastened with a bronze pin at his shoulder, hung down below his waist. He also wore a round, brimless hat and on his feet, a pair of very simple, leather sandals.

Emma, still scratching, wore a short green tunic that reached down to her waist, with roughly cut sleeves covering her upper arms. Where the tunic left off at her waist, a short skirt of similar colour hung to just above her knees. The skirt was made of heavy cloth and tassels, whereas the rest of her clothing, like William's, was made of primitively woven sheep's wool mixed with rather scratchy animal hair.

"I feel like a tramp," Emma said.

"Well, just pray you have a tramp's good sense," the case retorted. "Do you know why the cat crossed the road? Because it was the chicken's day off!"

"Don't listen to it, Emms. Hopefully, we don't have to stay here long."

As they moved closer, William could discern that the

houses on the hill fort were circular hut-like structures, seemingly made of upright wooden posts linked together with woven sticks. All had low-pitched roofs of thatch. There was one house, however, that appeared to be larger than the rest. It had a squat wooden tower of about fifteen to twenty feet.

William gazed all around. He pointed to a place a few yards away from the hill. "I suppose that's where Edras's village will be in 1066," he said thoughtfully.

Suddenly, there was a vague, far-off rumble from the direction of the depths of the forest.

"What was that?" Emma stopped.

"Your stomach bubbling probably, lumpkin!" the case commented testily.

The children carried on, walking a little way until William halted. He heard the sound of rumbling again. It was definitely getting nearer and clearer.

"Go down on your stomach, Emms." He pulled her down. "Something's coming, I'm sure of it. We mustn't be seen until we know what it is. The low bushes in front should keep us from view."

William was wise to be cautious, for not long after, the rumbling became a menacing rhythm of wheels and hooves and the stirring in the grass became voices that didn't sound friendly at all.

Out of the forest, four chariots came racing with the sound of rumbling thunder as they trailed shadows behind them. These were followed by nine horse riders, hard hooves scattering bushes and thistle seeds. After these, there came thirty or so armed men on foot. They came charging into the clearing, then turned.

Each chariot was a large two-wheeled cart, with heavy wicker basketweave sides, rising in a semicircle, pulled by a pair of dark horses. Each pair was held by a single wooden shaft lying between them, the end of the shaft being attached to a yoke that lay over the horses' shoulders and was kept in place by girths and straps around the horses' necks. Each chariot carried a crew of two. One to drive and the other....the other! Well, what about the other?

William scanned his eyes around the scene. He just couldn't believe what he saw. The four drivers were human but the four warriors in the chariots were very, very peculiar indeed. Their faces, such as William could see in the distance, were scaly and their skin was tinged distinct shades of green. They seemed about five foot high but as broad as they were tall. In their strange silver tunics, they gave the overall appearance of immense toads standing upright.

"Wh...what are they, Billy?" Emma was wide-eyed with disbelief.

"No idea, Emms! They might be goblins, like those I've read of in my *Brothers Grimm* books. They look almost exactly as I imagined goblins would. I've seen several drawings of them. But whatever they are, they're certainly not paying a friendly visit to the hill."

The soldiers were wearing helmets with crude wings on the side and black tunics with large bronze-studded belts of leather, which held swords with curved blades that split, at about six inches from the tip, to form two savage points. They also had triangular shields that bore the motif of a large black bird. As well as these, the horse soldiers carried spears with three heads glinting to reveal furrows in their metal; in these furrows was deadly poison.

The chariots spread out at the foot of the hill, eight men behind each. The horse soldiers manoeuvered to complete the semicircle.

A noise was coming from the village. William recognised this noise; it was the sound of frightened havoc. One of the toad-creatures made a sign. But suddenly, from the top rampart of the hill, thirty or more men, wearing tunics similar to William's, emerged carrying javelins, slings, and bows and started firing upon the attackers below. One villager shouted:

"Turn back Istarim and take your demons with you!"

Before the stones, arrows, and spears could find their targets, the four toad-creatures raised their arms, and from a short black rod that each was holding, came a searing blue-white light that shot up and consumed the approaching projectiles; leaving, within a second, simply a thin fall of harmless dust.

"Crimney!" William gasped. Emma clung to her brother.

Some of the villagers were obviously affected like the children and they fled back. But others retaliated immediately by discharging their missiles. These were also changed to dust. To avoid being disintegrated as well, these villagers fled. This had the desired effect, for, with the ensuing commotion, the remainder fell back to their houses.

The goblins, as William was now sure they were, destroyed the first ramparts, then the second, and then the last. They gurgled out a command. With vicious cries and shrieks, their soldiers brandishing weapons clambered up to the village on top of the hill.

It seemed all was lost. Then, just as they were at the brow, an old man came forward and stood bent but adamant in their way; stemming the onslaught.

"Stay thy wickedness!" He pointed a warning finger at them. "I am Alfgar, Bretwalda of this region and Thain Adviser to High Chieftain Pentrigan. Thou shalt not take this, my village, into bondage."

"Old fool," shouted one of the Istarim soldiers. Before Alfgar could respond, three poisoned javelins flew at him. Hurriedly he put his hands to his head, and, in deep concentration, said some words that sounded to William like magic. A whirling wind slowed the javelins down and the three deadly darts sank harmlessly into the ground at the old man's feet.

Amazed, the enemy backed away slightly.

"Return from here to your foul mines you Istarim, and take the devil Jinntars with you. Tell them to return to their land above the clouds!" Alfgar boomed, "Or feel the magic power of Mona!"

The enemy looked back at the toad-creatures as if asking what should be done. Their answer came both bright and cruel. Four light rays shot up, burning brands of white fire. Where old Alfgar had once stood, only a swirl of dust the size of a man remained, momentarily, before being carried on its final journey by the west wind. The magician was gone. A wind that seemed to bemoan its going.

There was no mourning at Algar's going, but cries of triumph from the attackers ensued as they mounted the hill's top and smashed into the village. The terrible cries of the village people filled the air as they fled through the back gates and blindly ran away. Williams and Emma screwed up their eyes and covered their ears, waiting for the attack to be over.

Soon it was. William took one hand off his ear and opened one eye. Then he opened both and prodded Emma. They watched the invaders taking their captives - the men, women, and children who were unable to flee - down from the village which was in ruins. Once at the foot of the hill, the horse soldiers, who had dismounted in readiness, placed neck-rings and iron chains around the captives, linking what must have been fifty to sixty people together.

One of the toad-creatures gave a sign, another shouted an order. Turning the chariots about, the grim procession went, like some snake of bad omen, back into the depths of the great oak forest.

Where the village had once been, beyond the broken ramparts and churned up soil, there were only flames flickering.

"Poor, poor people," Emma cried. "Their homes are

gone and they are prisoners."

"I'm beginning to think the past is a very dangerous place indeed. That, or the case is deliberately putting us into troubled times to put me off returning it. Well, it won't work. My mind's made up." William paused and scratched his chin. "Um! However, I must admit I don't quite know what to do now."

He got up on one knee and scanned warily round. The rumbling that had been rapidly receding now vanished altogether. Where chaos had descended so swiftly, now only silence and the sound of crackling flames, took its place.

"Perhaps, though I dread to say so, the case can shed some light on our darkness." But, when William looked, he found it annoyingly conspicuous by its absence.

"Nuisance!" William muttered. "Well, we're on our own. I presume that means that someone must still be about and that's where the case will be. I'll go and investigate. Emms, you stay here and keep cavey, those goblins may be somewhere near still, and…."

"Don't bother going on, Billy. I'm coming with you."

"Oh, alright. I really can't judge what the best course of action is. Let's just traipse forward carefully."

So, slowly, and very, very cautiously, the two children approached the crushed hill fort. They started the climb. When they reached the top, the sight they saw was awful. Emma closed her eyes.

The round huts had been broken, some partially changed into dust. What appeared to be wood-lathes and looms were smashed. Some bronze pots were broken, contents spilt everywhere. It was as though a tornado had mercilessly swept through. There were no signs of life or even bodies. Anything that moved had been captured and taken.

William sighed and not too hopefully called out, "Is there anybody here? Can anyone hear me?"

There was a rustle.

With more hope, "Is anybody there?" William was sure there was. "Emms, open your eyes. Someone's here; keep a look out."

"Yes, Billy."

"There is somebody here, isn't there? Please answer, we're friends," William stressed.

After an anxious moment, a figure came up from a hole that had been covered by a straw-camouflaged trapdoor behind a large, broken loom. The figure stepped past a bronze cauldron, brandishing a large knife. It was a boy, probably a year or two older than William, dressed in similar clothing who had a muddy red color. Around his neck, he wore a bronze torque.

"Who are you?" the boy said gruffly, holding up his knife. "Are you Istarim or Mona?"

"We're friends," William said diplomatically. "I'm William and this is my sister, Emma."

For a tense moment, the three stood like statues, stiff with indecision.

"Are you Arob Naq?" William asked at last.

"Are you of the tribe of Mona?" the boy asked.

William took a chance: "Yes, yes we are."

"But Billy..." Emma stopped, realising her brother had to give an answer.

"I am Arob," the boy said, "though I do not know why you call me Naq. That is the royal name and I am not royalty."

"Just Arob. Oh, I see!" William began to realise that he had found the wrong person.

"Yes, I am Arob, acolyte of the Druid Alfgar of Barrowdip, whom the wicked Jinntars destroyed."

"Jinntars; are they the goblins?"

"Goblins?"

"The toad-like creatures."

"Yes," Arob said, "the evil toad-creatures from above the clouds."

"We saw the attack; it was horrid," Emma said sympathetically.

The boy looked at her and put away his knife.

"Which village do you come from?" he asked.

William thought quickly, "It was destroyed by these Jinntars. We...we escaped and have wandered for days."

"Yes, the Jinntars with their lackeys, the Istarim, appear to be invincible." Arob sighed. "Ever since they came from their land above the clouds six moons ago, village after village of the Mona people has fallen, as well as hill forts, lake dwellings, and three Broch. The only thing that can be said for the accursed Jinntars is that they harm as few people as possible, but that is only because they need prisoners to do work; though for what I am not entirely certain."

"It is very strange," William agreed.

"And now High Chieftain Pentrigan Naq is in the gravest danger because Alfgar, the last and greatest of his advisers, is gone. If Pentrigan Naq falls, after all the defeats we have suffered before, the whole of the Mona people will lose heart and bow the knee to the conqueror. Already the Jinntars are spreading their influence. I was Alfgar's acolyte, but I have not yet mastered the ancient arts of the Druids that would let me help my people."

"Who are the Istarim?" William wanted to know as much as possible.

"You don't know?" Arob's voice was suddenly suspicious. "Your village must have indeed been isolated! The human Istarim are the invaders, who came long ago from across the Vast Water. They live in nomadic groups in the forests. They do not farm, only fight and plunder. Our forts held them in check until the coming of the non-human devilish Jinntars."

"Billy," Emma said, tugging anxiously at his tunic, "do please let's leave this place. I don't like it."

"The girl speaks strangely, but true. It would be best to

87

be gone; the village stinks of defeat."

With a balefully forlorn last look around, Arob went with the two children. They slowly climbed down the hill from where the village had once stood and walked, in silence, a little way across the open. William was weighing up in his mind if the case had played another trick on him and had taken him to the wrong Arob.

"Be more specific," William muttered to himself, mockingly imitating the case's voice.

"Well, I do not know where we should go," Arob said thoughtfully. "There is no safety anywhere; except perhaps the Broch of Pentrigan Naq and that is miles from here."

"Arob," William paused, then continued cautiously, "do you know anything about a silver case?"

"Silver case?" the boy said blankly. "What do you mean?"

"Oh, that stupid case!" Emma moaned.

"Case, what is this case?" Arob asked again.

"Oh, it's of no importance," William said as nonchalantly as he could. "It's just a trinket that I lost. I…. I was wondering if someone had found it." This didn't sound too convincing, so he added urgently, "I think it would be best if we head for Pentrigan, as you said." Perhaps Arob Naq will be there, he added to himself.

But Arob had ceased listening. He turned and suddenly drew his knife.

"Oh, dear!" Emma exclaimed, startled.

"Wh…what's the matter?" William asked anxiously.

"Look yonder," Arob pointed. "Quickly, my friends, we are in mortal danger."

William looked round. In the distance, he saw three fierce, mounted figures.

In the blink of a frightened eye, they had spurred their horses and were charging towards the children.

11

Be On Your Star Guard

Hooves thundered the horses forward. The grim, merciless faces grew more distinct and terrible at the approach.

"Oh Billy, I want to go home," Emma cried. "I want to go home."

Her brother grabbed her hand.

"We must run, or be lost forever," Arob urged.

And run they did. They ran and ran with leg-aching speed, to the awful sound of the horses galloping in pursuit. Louder and louder they sounded until the snorting of the Istarium's mounts seemed to shiver down their sweating necks.

Arob held tightly onto his knife. The forest appeared so far away. Before they could reach any cover, one of the horsemen overtook them, bringing the children's dash for safety to a sudden halt. The other two horsemen flanked them. They were well and truly caught.

One, with black eyes and eyebrows that bristled like sharks' teeth across his forehead, drew his sword.

"So! More little diggers for us, eh!" he growled.

"Yes, Brandicca, a fine catch."

"Rogg will be well pleased," another hissed.

"Not for Rogg," Brandicca said grimly with a cutting look in his sharp eyes, "but for Brandicca, and don't you forget it, Dradidda." He grabbed William by the scruff of his neck and raised him to his horse. Dradidda grasped Emma and hoisted her onto his mount. Both struggled, but to no avail.

"Let go of us," William gasped and would have thought, 'Here we go again,' if he hadn't been so worried. Emma just cried, it was all rather too much for her to take, and who could blame her?

But, Arob had his knife at the ready. As the third Istarim attempted to lay hold of him, he lunged forward and spun away from him with amazing agility.

"Ha!" Brandicca laughed. "Can't even handle a boy, Sambraticca?"

"You'll perish for that, brat," Sambricca screamed at Arob. Pulling the knife out from his hand, the Istarim swung his sword down at the boy. Arob leapt back from the deadly swing of the double-tipped blade and raised his hands chanting:

Earth Mother breathe deliverance upon your faithful son;

Let the evil that is here, be now undone.

Although these words were not English, by some magic, William could understand every one.

Suddenly, a great wind whisked along and, gaining strength, it caught Sambraticca's horse, causing it to rear up and send the Istarim crashing to the ground.

"Witch-child," snarled Dradidda. Holding Emma with one hand, he drew his weapon with the other. He charged at Arob, who avoided being hit but fell into the arms of Sambraticca who, having quickly recovered, held him in a painful, steely grip.

"Your devilry shall not save you now," yelled Dradidda, raising his sword.

"No!" Emma screamed.

But it was too late.

Just as Dradidda was going to grab hold of Arob, a golden beam shimmered strongly into the Istarim. He halted exactly where he was, as stiff as a statue, glowing a golden colour.

"What demonry is this?" gasped Sambraticca, throwing Arob to the ground.

Brandicaa, who still held William, turned his steed about and galloped off at full pace in the opposite direction.

"Come back with my brother," Emma cried, getting off the horse; for only Dradidda had been affected by the beam.

By now, Sambricca was beside himself with confused fury. With sword flashing, he lunged at Arob, the blade slashing a deep scratch in his arm, as he rolled aside.

"No more of your magic!" Sambricca screamed and raised his sword to strike again. Emma ran to try and help Arob, but before she reached him, another golden beam shot out and froze the remaining Istarim.

Arob breathed a heavy sigh of relief, but Emma cried out as she caught the final sight of Brandicca with his captive, disappearing into the thick foliage of the anonymous forest.

"Why didn't you use your golden power to save my brother?" she sobbed.

"It was not I who caused that magic, young friend," said Arob. "Even the Earth Mother has not such immediate and unusual power."

"Then what was it?" Emma stared at the glowing figures of the two stiff Istarim.

"I know not!" Arob sounded just as puzzled as she was.

"Have no dread," a rather loud, though beautiful voice proclaimed.

The children turned round very quickly, and....sheer amazement. Coming towards them was the most curious figure that either of the children, despite their very different backgrounds and experiences, had ever seen. He was a giant of a man, some eight to nine feet in height, quite slimly built, with golden skin, and a great head of curling golden hair. He was very handsome, although one was distracted from gazing at his features by the large golden ring that rotated anti-clockwise just above his head.

He was wearing a one-piece suit of gold, giving the effect of almost being part of his shimmering skin. Somehow, his very being seemed to radiate peace.

As he approached, Emma could see that on each wrist and on each ankle, he had a small pair of golden wings, about the size of those of a nightingale.

"A god!" Arob exclaimed breathlessly, getting down on bended knees. "Praise the god, girl, or he will smite us as well."

Emma just stood dumbfounded. After all, it isn't every day that you meet a god, now is it! No, of course not.

The giant gave a short laugh. "Please raise yourself. This praise is rather embarrassing," he said. It was then Emma saw that although the giant spoke with a deep musical voice; in fact, he had no mouth. The sound came solely from the rotating golden ring. But Arob refused to raise himself. He merely supplicated himself more.

"Please," the golden figure said; if you could say 'said' since it was the ring that seemingly spoke, "I am no god. I am Mercurio Nine of the Star Guard. Stop lying down so."

Emma put her head to one side, wondering what on earth he was talking about. But it wasn't anything 'on earth' at all.

"I have just arrived on your planet after tracking these nefarious Jinntars across twelve Star Systems."

"He *is* a god," Arob kept insisting.

"I admit I would have liked to have been a deity; my father would have cared greatly for that. But really, I would never have passed the finals." Mercurio's voice was very matter-of-fact. "Now you will please raise yourself, young Earth-man."

It was finally beginning to sink in. Arob rose to his feet.

"I am what you might call a policeman," Mercurio said, "of the intergalactic variety, naturally."

"A policeman!" Emma said in disbelief. "Sergeant Treadmill, back at my home, looks nothing at all like you."

Arob looked more and more puzzled.

"I've been after Grimston Rogg and his wicked crew for almost an eon; tracking them from their own planet Weebil One to Sonartario to Dentull Rota and finally to this small tucked-away place. Here, I shall at last, take them back to their just desserts on Belaqua Beta; the planet of justice."

"I still don't understand, really!" Emma was completely flummoxed. "What are these horrid Jinntars? And why are they here? And....and what about Billy? What are you going to do about my brother?"

"Now, little one, calm yourself," Mercurio began in a soothing tone. "The Jinntars are for the most part a very civilised race."

"They are Warriors of evil," Arob interrupted bitterly, "enemies of all that is good; enemies of the Mona people."

"Please, allow me to finish," Mercurio insisted pleasantly, but firmly. "The Jinntars, as I have stated, live on Weebil One, which is just inside the next galaxy from here; turn left at Alpha Centuri and carry on a little way. As races go, they are quite advanced and show respect for the Universal Council. Grimston Rogg and his bad band, however, are criminals in the first degree. He knows the cost of everything, the value of nothing. For many cycles, he has searched planets for precious metals to mine, so that he may grow wealthier and wealthier and thus more powerful. Rogg invariably picks a backward, 'closed' planet such as this, where he will not meet too much resistance and where he feels hidden from any Star Guard patrols. He steals as much of the population as he needs to carry out his mining operations."

"That is what he is doing here." Although Arob didn't understand much of what Mercurio was saying, he knew instinctively it was the truth.

"Yes. And, I'm afraid to say he has struck lucky, for he has found what you call tin; the rarest, most valued metal in his sector of Alpha Centuri. With it, he will be able to buy the services of the fighting mercenaries of Astaria. He has had the desire to do this for a long, long time. It will enable him to overthrow his brother Tyron Kragg, who is Presider of Weebil One, and then declare himself ruler of his world and its two dominion planets."

"This is so strange. Yet, Alfgar said I should listen to everything new," Arob said. "For he told me there would come a time when a sign would be revealed and I would fulfill the Earth Mother's destiny for me. Perhaps all that has happened is that sign."

Emma just sighed. "I'm so worried about Billy," she said anxiously.

"I shall retrieve your brother little earth-child," Mercurio reassured her. "My scanners have traced the place where the Jinntars have hidden their ship. I shall fix onto that. From there I shall be able to discover where their main mine camp is."

"Please, do start soon," Emma urged.

"Wait young Earthman," Mercurio said, "you are hurt." He had seen Arob's cut.

"It is nothing but a scratch," he answered. "I cut it on a rock when I rolled away from the Istarim." But, immediately, a tiny beam shot down from Mercurio's halo and the cut disappeared as if it had never existed.

"Oh, do let's go now," Emma disregarded Arob's comments of amazement.

"No little one," Mercurio said firmly, "you and he must go to the nearest place of safety. What I must do, I can do far faster alone."

"But, great one," Arob said earnestly, "the nearest place is the Brock of Pentrigan. It is miles away."

"You have two mounts," Mercurio suggested. Indeed, perhaps stunned by the freezing of their masters, the two horses had remained, calmly grazing. "I will give you protection," Mercurio added. "I was given this some time ago but have not used it; such trifles do not amuse me. I have redirected most of its power as an extra security device against prisoner break-outs on board my ships."

As if from nowhere, he produced the case. Emma gasped in shock, she had completely forgotten about it.

Mercurio gave it to Arob, after having touched it with one of his beams. "Take this," he said. "I have programmed it to protect you. It's like a power pack. But you must not open it, for then it reverts to being a 'Prize,' and will no longer offer you protection."

"But....but you can't give it to him," Emma said, but before she could explain, Mercurio floated up, his small golden wings flapping.

"Good speed for your journey," he said. "Remember – do not open the case."

He seemed to run on air. In a matter of moments, he had disappeared into the forest.

Arob figured the case as he stared at it. Emma gazed at him, new worries entering her head. Destiny was taking its course. Without William she could not wish herself back to her time; the case only took wishes from her brother. She was stuck and if anything happened to her brother, then she would be stranded in this time for good. She would have begun to feel miserable, but she had no time. The two Istarim suddenly stopped glowing golden. As the beam wore off, they moved with furious faces.

"So, you thought to make clods of Dradidda and Sambraticca," said Sambraticca, gazing through dark, unreflective buzzard's eyes. "You shall pay with your lives.

Your golden guardian is gone. Nothing can save you now. Dradidda, take the girl."

The two split up. Each drew a dagger that glinted menacingly in the early morning sun. Sambricca growled like a rabid dog and jumped at Arob. Immediately, the Istarim was thrown backward and changed into a baaing sheep, happy to sniff the native air on his own ground. Dradidda gazed at this transformation aghast. He let go of Emma and started running away. Before he had covered ten yards, instead of two feet touching the ground, four hooves slowed down, and the once vicious mouth started 'baaing' along with his fellow before fancying some grass and grazing contentedly. For Dradidda was now also a sheep.

"Goodness!" exclaimed Emma.

"How did all this happen?" Arob was astonished.

"All part of the service; we aim to please. I was going to share some sheep humor but decided it was too baaaaaaad!" said the case. "Mind you, I could be of far greater assistance if that intergalactic spoilsport hadn't decided to rearrange my Domwangler. Now, worthy, if you merely open me, my Domwangler will return to normal."

"Don't listen to it," Emma pleaded. "Mercurio warned you not to open the beastly thing."

"He did. I shall not abuse his trust," Arob replied, rather surprised that the case could talk, though growing accustomed to the unusual!

"Your wits have gone wool-gathering. Still, I think you shall soon see reason," said the case knowingly.

Emma stared at Arob. "So you are the First-Given," she said, "though I cannot see why you aren't called Arob Naq!"

"I suggest, old chap," said the case, ignoring her, "you commence your little journey. There's only trouble for you here and it's a long walk to safety."

"Walk!" Arob looked around. "You've changed the horses into sheep as well!"

"You *are* a stupid thing," Emma complained.

"A mistake, dumbo. I was not created as a security device," the case retorted. "I'm sure that if somebody wanted to use you as a safety-pin, you wouldn't be very good; although you wouldn't yap, yap so much, which would be better!"

"I do not know about any of this," Arob said firmly, "but we must go away from here now."

And so, with four sheep baaing and grazing gently in the field, Emma and Arob started off towards the Broch of Pentrigan on foot.

Somehow his very being seemed to radiate power and peace.

And so, with four sheep baaing and grazing gently in the field,
Emma and Arob started off to the Broch of Pentrigan on foot.

12

Mine and Them and Mercurio

The ride was like being tied by your stomach to a spring and then bounced against bags filled with rocks. William felt very, very miserable.

As they rode deeper into the forest, which seemed to go on forever, William could only see the mossy floor as Brandicca kept cursing and threatening to do the most terrible things to him. "I shall spit-roast you over a slow-burning fire," was one of his favorite threats and, what it lacked in imagination, it made up for in nastiness.

They passed six or seven Istarim standing guard. Stretching his head up, William could make out some cliffs in the distance.

Still, they bumped on, his stomach aching as if it had a large wooden splinter in it. At last, they approached a huge wooden gate, set in a high wooden barricade.

"Open them!" Brandicca shouted. Two Istarim opened the gates. They rode through.

Brandicca drew his horse to a halt. Pushing William down onto the ground, he jumped down himself. William rolled over, rather dazed. Looking hurriedly around, William saw he was in a large clearing in which there appeared to be mineworkers moving in and out of an opening in a hill. Lines of men, women, and children were carrying loads out of the mine; others laden with hammers and spades were heading into the mine. They were guarded by several grim-faced, well-armed Istarim. A Jinntar was giving orders.

"Fetch Captain Conicubbicca!" Brandicca shouted putting one foot on William. "Tell him Brandicca has brought some more mine-fodder." He laughed gruffly and pressed his foot down harder on William's side.

"Stop that!" William cried.

"'Stop that!' eh, devil-child, your magic won't stop you from working in the mine or being extinguished when you can no longer work. All this land will be the Istarim's when the Jinntars have taken what they want." Then he added, under his bitter breath, "Or maybe even before."

A large man with a tremendous black beard came striding over. "So, you have another, Brandicca. Well, let him up. He's only a boy. There is no need to cause him any more pain."

That's rich! William thought. 'Save his strength for the mine.' William was certain that's what he meant.

"You are too soft with the accursed Mona people, Cognicubbicca," Brandicca sneered. They exchanged hateful looks.

"Save your lip," Cognicubbicca hissed. He looked round. "Where are Dradidda and your *dear* brother Sambraticca?"

"Trouble," Brandicca snorted, roughly pulling William to his feet. "Something to do with this brat. A golden beam appeared from nowhere; they went stiff."

"Golden beam!" the voice was horribly high-pitched and gurgling. William watched a toad-creature half-walk, half-hop into view. "Golden beam you say? Did you see where it came from?"

"No," Brandicca replied gruffly.

The Jinntar stared at William with its large green slit eyes. Then, it stomped off, over to a large round wooden building.

"I'll put him straight to work," Brandicca snarled.

Cognicubbicca grunted and walked off. It was obvious there was no love lost between them, only stored hate that seemed as if it might explode at any time.

Brandicca dragged William over to three Istarim who instructed him on the very arduous work that he had to do....or else!

"Right! In you go, maggot!" Brandicca pushed him into a dejected line of others trudging into the side of the hill.

"Hold!" A particularly nasty, gurgling voice grated into William's ears like chalk scraped across a blackboard. Brandicca pulled him out from the line that continued on its way into the darkness of the mine.

William looked round and cringed. He saw a Jinntar, larger and uglier than the rest; its green, scaly skin tinged with black-raised veins. It was wearing a long purple tunic with the design of a hideous black bird on the front. On its big, flat, green head it wore a square copper crown studded with tin. It wore this as if greater than all else, for this was Grimstom Rogg's, head of the Jinntars, most precious possession.

"Is this the new one, Brandicca?" Rogg gurgled.

"Yes." For once William detected a note of obedience in Brandicca's usually defiant voice.

"So, I have been told that a golden beam saved your friends." Rogg glowered at William, who swallowed fearfully. "Answer!" Rogg demanded.

"Y....yes."

"Sooooo, who wielded the weapon, eh?"

"I....I don't kn...know." William was sweating profusely.

"Was it a Star Guard? Was it? Was it?" His voice was playfully malicious. He tickled William's chin with a long, green, webbed finger that sported a sharp, jagged nail at the end. "Was it, Earth slime?"

"H....honestly, I....I don't know." William attempted to

keep a whimper of despair out of his voice. 'Remember.' he thought, 'in the darkest of times, the candle of hope still burns.'

"If you are lying," Rogg gurgled viciously, "you shall feel the thousand terrors of the screaming darkness that knows no end, and then it will get a lot worse!" He shook a long fingernail at William with deliberate menace and darted its sharp, jagged nail so close to the petrified boy's left eye that William thought that he was going to do something really horrible. He recoiled in horror. Rogg laughed and moved grotesquely away.

"Right, Mona-brat, in you go," Brandicca snarled when Rogg was well out of earshot. "Now that the hideous toad has gone, you can work your fingers off in the darkness." Brandicca shoved him into the next line with the rest and William shuffled along into the mine. As he walked further into the damp, musky darkness, William heard Rogg shout, "Istarim that are not on guard duty, prepare to march on the Broch of Pentrigan. We must act quickly now. Agrog and you two stay here. Watch over them, Brandicca. You stay here and keep order in your people. Captain Cognicubbicca, prepare the chariots. If there is a Star Guard this close on my track, I want to be the first to 'greet' him."

Now, a lot of this didn't make sense to William but it made him even more worried about his sister and himself.

"Hallo," said a soft voice next to him. "Who are you? I am Dianta."

It was very dark in the mine, only torches of wood served to give any light. Even so, William could see that there were many others working away at the hard rocks. He could discern in the flickering, half-light that the voice near him belonged to a young girl; possibly about his age. She appeared to have long dark hair and a rather pretty face.

"I'm William."

"That is a good name," she said.

"Shut it! Work!" shouted a harsh guard. The girl touched William's hand gently with hers, as if in reassurance. Together they dug with their hands and rough tools into the tough stone. Work was done in silence, except for the occasional groans of men, women, and children – digging, digging, digging in the mocking dimness, under the severe gaze of five armed Istarim guards.

From the distance outside, William could hear the sound of many horses and chariots and feet leaving the mine camp with cries of battle. Above all was the evil, commanding voice of Grimston Rogg. Soon, the clatter of arms receded into the depth of the forest.

Time dragged. It seemed to William that he had been working for days, though it could have really only been for hours. Then:

"You, guard!" a rough voice said; it was Brandicca, "Now is the time to act. We no longer need the help of these Jinntars. Let us take the opportunity. The others are with me."

There were sounds of agreement.

"Good. Then this is what we'll do. There is only Agrog and the two other Jinntars here. We know they see badly in the dark. That is why they hardly ever enter the mine. So, we lure them in and then dispatch them before they have time to use their accursed weapons."

There was other talking that William couldn't quite overhear.

"What's happening?" Dianta asked.

"Nothing good," was William's hasty reply.

Brandicca moved to the entrance. "Quickly, Agrog!" he shouted. "We have discovered something that is more valuable than any other thing but we cannot bring it out. You must come in and see for yourself."

"Must I?" came the gurgling reply. "Very well."

Argog entered, followed by Brandicca, who drew a sword behind the Jinntar's back. The other Istarim made ready to strike. There was no need; in a flash of metal, Brandicca knocked Argog with the hilt and had him taken away and imprisoned.

There was a gasp from the mineworkers.

"Silence!" Brandicca hissed. "Or every one of you will meet the same fate." He knelt down and picked something up. "Ha, this is it," he said, holding up a black rod with a luminous green band in the middle. "The Jinntar's power-rod. With it, I will be the ruler of all."

The guards shuffled uneasily.

"Any objections?" he said threateningly, waving the rod in front of them.

"No...no, Brandicca. You are the chieftain now," they said fearfully.

Hearing the noise, the two other Jinntars came in. Brandicca jumped out at them, brandishing his weapon. "Drop your rods," he said, "or I'll blast you."

"Go ahead," gurgled one of the Jinntars.

"What!" Brandicca screamed. "You want this? Well, so be it!"

He squeezed the luminous band as he had seen the Jinntars do. Sure enough, out came a searing white-blue light that lit up half the mine. But instead of hitting the two Jinntars, it smashed into Brandicca, who immediately swirled away in a cloud of sparkling dust.

"Ha!" laughed the Jinntar. "Don't you see the joke, you savages? He had the rod the wrong way round – we could see that all the time. Ha, ha!"

The other Jinntar laughed as well and both opened fire on the five guards, who joined their leader in the Netherworld.

"Oh, no," Dianta whimpered and held tightly onto William.

"Pograt, you stay here whilst I get some more watchers for these *sweet* little workers. Rogg will be well pleased with us stopping such an insurrection."

The Jinntar went out.

"Back to work!" yelled Pograt, brandishing his power-rod around the large mine.

All hope of freedom seemed to be falling away like grains of sand, slipping through tired hands. Wearily and helplessly, William went back to work.

Then, suddenly, instead of the guards returning, he heard sounds coming from outside. Sounds of commotion, cries of anger, the sound of swords being drawn. Then, silence.

Agitated, Pograt turned to see what was happening. In desperation, William grabbed a large stone and dropped it with a thud on the Jinntar's flat green foot. His screech was enough to shatter glass! Pograt staggered for a moment and then turned.

"You will pay for that, Earthling." But before he could act, several of the workers jumped on him. Then, they danced a merry dance as Pograt hopped, still holding his throbbing foot. They left him to his crazy jig.

"Right!" William said to all the workers. "Let's get out of here."

In a rush, they all streamed out of the mine. Instead of swords swinging around them from the fighting Istarim, as they had expected upon their emergence into the light, there was an incredible sight.

The Jinntar stood frozen in a golden glow and all the Istarim were on their bended knees, trembling as if they were in the presence of a god.

It was Mercurio. The Istarim who had not supplicated themselves had fled.

"Have no dread," Mercurio said. "Sorry that it took a long time getting here, but I had to liberate another mine as well as find Rogg's craft. Unfortunately, I have not discovered him as yet."

At these strange words, the Mona people also got down in reverence.

"Get down William," Dianta said, tugging at his tunic. "He is a god come to deliver us from bondage, as was foretold."

"Please raise yourselves," Mercurio urged. "I am no deity." He motioned them to rise and one by one, they did. "Well, if I were you, the first thing I should want to do is to celebrate freedom once again," Mercurio suggested.

In a flurry of joy, the Mona people cheered and hugged and thanked the Earth and thanked the Sky. They then turned bitter gazes at the forty or so Istarim remaining.

"Go," Mercurio said to the Istarim, "and never trouble these people again."

"Why let them go? Slay them," said some of the freed workers.

"No," replied the others. "Then we would be no better than they."

"You are wise," Mercurio said. "Let them go."

And they fled for all their lives were worth, which was probably not much, but they ran very quickly all the same!

"I seek one called William," Mercurio said.

Dianta looked at William, as though he was suddenly very important.

William stepped forward. "Do you know what has happened to my sister?"

"Yes. She is with the other boy," Mercurio replied. "They have gone to the safety of the Broch of Pentrigan."

"Oh, no," William gasped. "That's where those horrible toad-creatures have gone! Oh, crimney, what's going to happen to her? It's all that stupid case's fault!"

Mercurio looked puzzled for a moment. Then, "I must hurry," he said. "The sooner I capture Grimston Rogg, the sooner this mess will be cleared up."

To the astonishment of all around, he rose ten feet in the

air.

"Wait," William urged, "you must take me with you."

Dianta came forward and touched his shoulder. "Stay with us," she said.

"Listen to the girl," Mercurio advised. "You would only slow me down."

"But I have something very important to do. I'm not of this time at all. It's all to do with the silver case – the Prize."

"Prize, you say?" Mercurio lowered to the ground. "Well, very well. You must explain on the way." He knelt down. "Climb on my back."

Just as William did, Dianta rushed forward and planted a kiss on his cheek. He blushed profusely.

"Goodbye," she said sadly. "Goodbye."

"Right!" William said to all the workers. "Let's get out of here."

"Very well. You must explain on the way." Mercurio
knelt down. *"Climb on my back."*

13

A Fate Worse Than Destiny

Across clearings, in another part of the great forest where the trees donned with moss beards murmuring in the wind seemed like Druids of old quietly chanting, Emma and Arob, and of course the case, made their way towards Pentrigan's Tower. Despite the case's constant interruptions, they had fallen into conversation.

"So, you never knew who your parents were? They must have been simply horrid," Emma said sympathetically.

"Well, yes," Arob replied. "But Alfgar was like a father to me. He said that one day, when the time was right, a sign would come and I would know who they were. Of course I yearned to know, but in time I learnt just to obey Alfgar and listen to his teachings."

"I don't think that was right," Emma said thoughtfully.

"Ah, there was so much to learn, so very much and I am afraid that I have only gained a part of the knowledge I need. I must always seek for more, feeling a destiny calling me somewhere."

"Many seek not to find, but to forget," commented the case. "Mock destiny like a bad joke, some say; but in the end, it will have its way – tomorrow, or today."

"Don't pay attention to that stupid thing," Emma snapped.

"All your lives are written on the wind, which cries like a baby, forever newly born," the case muttered.

"Yes, Alfgar taught me much," Arob continued, throwing off the mood the case caused, "and I keep all this learning here and here." He pointed to his head and his heart. There was a vague frown on his dark features, "But only when I become a man will I truly know how and why I should use what I have learnt. If only it was sooner."

"Do you mean magic?" Emma asked.

"Not magic," he replied, "rather knowledge of how to be one with the great Earth Mother. Serve her well and she will serve you. Abuse her gift of nature and goodwill and she will strike back. It was not magic that caused those javelins to fall at old Alfgar's feet, but her breath catching them and placing them in her own breast rather than that of her servant's. I wanted to fight, but Alfgar had told me that above all I must not be captured and made me promise to hide. For the evil Jinntars are not of this Earth, but from the sky. It has been said that they came down from above the clouds in a great black raven. Even the Earth Mother's power cannot stop them."

"Ah, but allow me to suggest that I could, worthy," said the case confidently. "If you just open me and make a wish, I shall deliver the goods, post-haste. You *are* the First-Given of this world, you know."

"Stuff and nonsense," Emma said hurriedly. "His name isn't Naq. Arob you must not open it. It only causes mischief."

"The last time I saw a mouth as big as yours, someone was riding behind it, clinker-brain," snapped the case. "You're as thick as plum-pudding. If I'm used 'properly' then no harm can come. My gyrating Domwangler will see to that."

"Please, Arob, don't believe it," Emma pleaded.

Arob made no reply.

They walked on through the fluttering shade of sun-clad

trees, in silence.

When they rested, Emma gazed up at the colours webbed between those tall trees and felt increasingly worried about her brother.

Arob leant up against a tree, about four yards from her. He held the case, "Can you grant me any wish?" he asked.

"Oh, tara-diddle," replied the case enticingly. "Why not press my button and see?"

But Arob remembered what Mercurio had said and so refrained from pressing the little purple button. Yet, even so, the case could tell by the strange gleam in the boy's eyes that he had made an impression.

After their brief rest, Arob and Emma walked on for hours. Both were growing very, very weary.

"Getting tired are we?" Well, that's your choice, isn't it? Take a rest; press my Domwangler and all will be well. It's your fate, Arob, my lucky lad," the case cajoled. "Yes, fate slaps some people on the back and some in the face. Even so, what will be will be and you can't break out from it. Catch my drift?"

"Oh, what are you talking about? It's clear as sunlight. You simply get worse and worse," Emma complained.

"Sunlight travels faster than sound; that's why you appear bright until you open your mouth," the case snapped indignantly. "I was just trying to tell you, young master, that *I* am your destiny. The 'fateful' sign Algard told you about."

"You *are* not!" Emma said firmly.

"I do not understand what you say," Arob said. "And you, Emma, I have seen that you have known this case before. You are not of my people, are you? Who are you? Where do you come from?"

"Ah-ha! Answer that if you can, muggins," the case mocked.

Emma was lost for words. "Well…." she began.

Suddenly Arob touched her shoulder. "Be silent," he

said in a strong voice.

It seemed to Emma as though a frightened whisper quivered through the leaves.

"Wh....what is it?"

"Can you not hear it, behind us, not far away," Arob whispered. "A noise, as of many people coming."

Even the trees seemed to draw near in fear.

"Quickly," Arob urged. "We must run."

And run they did, although they were tired. They rushed through the tall trees with some terrible feeling closing in on them. Emma tried her best to keep up with Arob, but every so often, he had to fall back to keep pace with her.

"You'll both need to run faster than that," the case advised, matter-of-factly.

But there came a time soon, when, out of breath and with a fast-beating heart, Emma just fell down and could run no more.

"I...I just can't go on," she cried.

"Do not worry," Arob said, stopping as well. "We will stand our ground. It might be friends."

"I wouldn't bank on it if I were you, buffo," the case said, frankly.

Soon, a great rushing clamour filled their ears. In the distance, gaining all the time, they could see the forces of Grimston Rogg approaching; charging towards them. The Jinntars were cutting a path through the forest with their disintegrator rods. Trees cringed into dust.

"We will never reach safety before they are upon us," Arob said. "We are doomed."

Chapter 14

Two Steps Forward (Three Backwards?)

He pressed the button.

"I wish we were in Broch Pentrigan." And….

Before Emma could say, "Oh, no!" - They were.

At least Arob was; Emma found herself precariously perched on a wooden ledge some thirty feet above the ground. Her head was reeling for she couldn't abide heights.

"I'm going to fall," Emma managed to gasp as she felt herself about to plunge earthward.

Just as her feet slipped, just as she expected to fall, two strong hands grabbed hold of her, pulling her inside to safety.

"Are you alright?" Arob asked, still holding her.

"Y….yes." She was still shaking. "I...it's all that stupid case's fault, as usual!"

"People who jump to conclusions, rarely land properly," the case said indignantly. "Gratitude is like a three-course meal to a hungry man; thanks for the popcorn!"

"Who is this?" a deep voice asked. It came from a very tall, broad man wearing a three-pronged bronze crown on his head of thick greyish hair. He had on a long tunic of green and a large leather belt, studded with bronze. A long green cloak billowed out behind him as he entered the room.

"Hold!" he commanded. "What are you doing in my

private chamber?"

The room was quite small, with wooden walls. It contained only a rough low bed in the corner and a table and a large chair. On one of the walls, there hung a dried, red deerskin.

"High Chieftain Pentrigan Naq," Arob said in a whisper. Arob bowed, so Emma curtsied as she thought fitting.

"Who are you, boy? I recognise your face," Pentrigan said, one hand clutching the large hilt of the sword that hung on his side. "Tell me, or I shall have to take action that will be little to your liking."

"Don't be hasty, my lord. I am Arob of the village of Barrowdip."

"Alfgar's acolyte!" The High Chieftain was obviously surprised.

"You know of me, my lord?" Arob was puzzled.

"That is of no importance for the moment. Who is she and what brings you to this Broch?" Pentrigan frowned.

"She is my...my friend from a nearby village," Arob said. "The Jinntars and Istarim attacked us this very sun-up, taking all of our people."

"And Alfgar? What of Alfgar, boy?" Pentrigan said earnestly.

"He is no longer, my lord," Arob replied sadly. "Gone to take his rightful place at the great Sky Table to dine with his ancestors."

"And I don't know where Billy is," Emma said.

"Oh, use a modicum of intelligence," snapped the case. "Speak when you're spoken to, hodge-podge."

"Who said that?" Pentrigan asked. "I saw no mouth move."

"Oh, it's something... something that Arob learnt! Isn't it Arob?" Emma prodded him.

"My lord, there is no time for this discussion now." He

114

ignored Emma. "Even at this moment, the enemy are sweeping their way through the forest in great numbers. They will be down upon us soon."

"The news darkens evermore," Pentrigan sighed. "It may be the final blow of defeat to the Mona people." He turned and went hurriedly out.

"Where do you think he has gone?" Emma asked.

"To Tipperary," said the case sarcastically.

"Look there." Arob led her to the window. The High Chieftain walked below, over to the guards at the two gates.

The wooden tower stood in the middle of a circle, the wall of which was high wooden posts with a frame of battlements, behind a deep furrow. Between the wall and all around the tower were several houses similar to the ones in Burrowdip. Many people were coming out and listening to the words of Pentrigan Naq; words that the two children could not hear. Then, they saw him turn as men all around went to arm themselves.

Soon, Pentrigan strode back into the chamber with a most purposeful look on his rugged face; as if he had made a decision about something that had weighed on his mind for years. He came up to Arob and placed two large hands on the boy's shoulders.

"It has been a long time," Pentrigan began, "since I visited you as a baby. Alfgar told me of your progress. He was proud of you; remember that."

"Yes, my lord!" Arob was frankly confused.

"I must now tell you something that I made Alfgar swear on his troth never to reveal. The forces of evil will soon be upon us and with the powers so weighted against us, well..." He sighed and sat down. "We have been so abused that no glory can come in the end for we that are old. Yet, even so, I shall meet this onslaught head-on and whatever happens, I feel I shall not be taken alive. But you must go willingly, must bide your time; for you are the hope of the

Mona people."

"I do not understand, my lord."

"I must tell you Arob, that you are my grandson; blood of my blood, flesh of my flesh."

"Arob Naq!" Emma exclaimed, realising what this meant.

"Yes, little one," Pentrigan smiled at her. "Your mother, Arob, was my daughter, Emmanta. But when she married your father Rigan, Overseer of Greendell, I would have nothing to do with them. Rigan was a proud man, but not of Naq blood. Oh, I realise now the folly of this mood but wisdom often only comes with hindsight. However, your mother and father were as happy as two lovebirds in Greendell. Then, one day, the hideous Troll Griptear, took two children from Greendell to his cave by the great waterfall. Your father went after the wicked monster. He found his filthy liar. There they fought a battle that is still talked of and Rigan became a hero, though neither survived. Griptear gone for good. Rigan wounded, brought the children back and passed in the arms of Emmanta. Hard man as I was then, I still would not go to her. Oh, too late I heard that she had pined away; gone to join Rigan in the bowels of the great Sky-Hill. Then Alfgar told me that he discovered that my daughter had given birth to a son some months before. I went to see you and gave you into the care of Alfgar. He was to train you in the ways of Earth-Power until the time came when the Mona people would call upon you for help."

Arob just gazed at his grandfather. His stare was hard, as if weighing something up.

"Alas, that Alfgar is no more," Pentrigan sighed. "Now you must know Arob Naq, that I mean you to be my successor."

"I have no knowledge of chieftainship," Arob said harshly.

"Alfgar planted seeds of knowledge within you, more

than you suspect. They are growing all the time and soon shall reach fruition."

Suddenly a man entered. "My lord," he began, "the enemy has been sighted in the far distance. They are approaching in great numbers. The Jinntars in chariots are leading. The people are panicking."

"I must speak with them." Pentrigan rose and turned to Arob. "Wait here, my son. Remember my words." The two men strode out of the room and climbed down the ladders through two floors until they reached the ground.

"Well," Emma began, "at least you know who you are now, Arob."

"The First-Given," the case said pointedly.

"Yes," Arob replied bitterly, "so mysteries are solved with words." He despised the way Pentrigan had treated his parents and him.

"Oh yes," the case said, "all secrets can be solved. I recall a rather droll story about a man who, in the middle of the night, thought he had discovered the secret of the universe. He managed to open his eyes long enough to rapidly scribble the secret of the universe down on a piece of paper by his bedside. Then he promptly went back to sleep."

"What's so 'droll' about that story?" Emma said. Arob was deep in thought.

"I haven't finished, dumbo," the case retorted indignantly. "Anyway, when he woke up he was naturally filled with excitement. He grabbed the piece of paper on which he had written the secret of the universe and eagerly read. However, the only thing on it was 'I am a Sausage.' Ha-ha!"

"You're as daft as ever!" Emma said in a huff and walked over to the window. Below she could see Pentrigan talking to his people. From feelings of defeat, he seemed to have given them back a fighting spirit. But when Emma looked up, all her heart left her. She could see trees falling into pillars of mist that rose swirling from the chariot wheels and hooves of the fast-approaching enemy.

"Oh goodness," she cried, "the beastly creatures are here already."

Arob rushed over beside her. They watched as Rogg's forces emerged from the desecrated wood and charged towards the main gates. When they were about three hundred yards from them, they stopped, as a signal was given and the Istarim and Jinntars spread out in a huge semicircle.

"Earth-idiots," Rogg shouted, "if the Star Guard is within your puny walls, let him come out to face his fate."

Pentrigan, moving hurriedly, entered his tower and climbed to the very top. He stood upon the highest platform, showing himself clearly and fearlessly to the enemy below as he drew his pride about him like a cloak and his cloak about him like the chieftain he was.

"What is it you want, evil one?" he cried out defiantly.

"If the Star Guard is not with you, then you are lost," Grimston Rogg gurgled wickedly.

"Foolish toad-creature. Your words signify nothing. Go back into the foul belly of your filthy black bird where you belong. You do not frighten me. I will not bandy words with such a low creature as you. Leave or face my wrath."

Even Cognicubbicca had to marvel at Pentrigan's audacious behavior. But Rogg merely laughed horribly.

"You are the fool, *little* man," Rogg mocked. "I left you before because I considered you no hazard and as a favor to Cognicubbicca here who wished you to be free to witness the gradual defeat of all your people. Is that not so Captain?"

Cognicubbicca flashed Rogg a resentful stare.

Rogg laughed again. "Your future, Pentrigan, stands burning upon barricades of fire. You are as bad as my brother Tyron Kragg; don't you realise, idiot, heroes are finished; their swords rust and crumble as bats fill their decaying towers. You are finished!" The Jinntar knew only too well the

118

taunting language of fear.

Emma felt tears trickle down her cheeks. Arob stood erect, as if facing an on-coming tidal wave, which he knew, would sweep away all before it.

"No!" Pentrigan Naq boomed, "I will not allow you to leave us with a life that is a crime!"

"Try and stop me!" Rogg roared triumphantly. Immediately, a beam shot upwards, turning the platform upon which Pentrigan stood to dust.

"My people, obey the boy Arob Naq, for he is my grandson," he cried and began to fall.

Tears welled up in Arob's eyes as Pentrigan hit the ground.

Cognicubbicca looked grim with disapproval. He held his horse steady behind Rogg's chariot. "That was not nobly done," he said.

"Hold your moronic tongue," Rogg lashed with a liquid growl.

"He is going to destroy the tower," Arob said to Emma. "We must hurry down."

They climbed down the ladders and joined others who came out of its structure. Before the last people had emerged, seven beams from seven rods demolished the tower, trapping several people on its downfall.

Cognicubbicca frowned deeply. "This is cowardly," he said.

Rogg glared at him, "Are you daring to question my authority?"

The Istarim clutched the hilt of his sword, "Yes," he said.

"What's happening?" Emma asked.

"May I suggest you make a wish to remove yourself from this mess," the case suggested.

"I may not need to," Arob said to Emma as they stood together now on the battlements. "It seems that the enemy are arguing amongst themselves." Indeed, Emma could see the

119

field before her covered with the semicircle of the Istarim. The seven Jinntar chariots were arranged in a wedge shape behind the larger armed cart of the Grimston Rogg. Rogg was visibly arguing with a man mounted on a heavy warhorse.

"I have seen enough of this destruction," Cognicubbicca said vehemently. "I shall not be a party to any more wanton wrecking. Even though Pentrigan was my great enemy, I would never have been so cowardly as to dispatch him in this way."

"You're a fool," Rogg sneered, "and I have no time for fools." He raised his power-rod at Cognicubbicca. But the Istarim was swift. Having drawn his sword, he lopped off the webbed hand of the Jinntar leader. Rogg screamed in agony.

Immediately the other Jinntars produced their weapons. Before they could fire, dozens of Istarim fell upon each and overpowered them.

The Mona people cheered.

Cognicubbicca shouted out some order to his men. The Jinntars, including Grimston Rogg, were trussed up securely with a thick cord and then were placed in a circle in the middle of the field.

"People of Broch Pentrigan," the Istarim Captain shouted, "let there be an end to these demons' influence. We have been lulled by promises of riches that have not been given to us and, for that, the Istarim are losing the nobility that they are heir to. We have become mere lackeys. But no more, Mona people. We shall leave these for you to deal with. We shall return to our former ways."

"Wait," another Istarim with red hair cried. He rode up to Cognicubbicca. "I say we take this Broch and put the Mona people under our thrall. It is our right. We shall be the masters and mine for gold. The Jinntars will obey us then." There was a dangerous look in his eyes.

"Oh, Strabidicca, haven't you learnt anything? Conquest must be done according to some code."

"That is the old way, Cognicubbicca. We take what we can now. I say that mastery of all others but the Istarim is the only safe future; the Jinntars have shown us that." It seemed that many of the Istarim agreed. There was much arguing in the Istarim ranks.

"It seems that our fate is again uncertain," Arob said.

"Yes. One swallow doesn't make a summer. So make a wish," the case replied.

"No, you mustn't," Emma stressed.

Cognicubbicca and Strabidicca had engaged in a bitter fight. Amidst the uncertainty, Arob opened the case: "I wish that the Great Golden One would come to help us."

"Oh, no!" Emma gasped, realising too late what Arob had done.

However, Mercurio, with his cargo, William, was already coming into view.

"Billy!" Emma cried out happily.

The sight of Mercurio made both the Mona and the Istarim look up, aghast. Strabidicca took the opportunity of this distraction to attack Cognicubbicca.

"T...traitor," Cognicubbicca gasped.

"Fool, I am the victor. That is all that matters. Your code of honour is a thing of the past. Go and join your 'beloved' Pentrigan and talk of old times in the Netherworld."

He kicked his horse and Cognicubbicca fell to the ground.

"Come," Strabidicca cried, "let us fight this Golden One."

Grimston Rogg saw his opportunity. "Istarim, release me and my fellows and we will help you overcome all."

"Yes," Strabidicca said, jumping down from his horse. He went over to release the Jinntars.

Some of the Istarim, those who supported Congicubbicca, picked up their wounded captain and rode away into the forest. No one stopped them; they were staring

121

warily at Mecurio's arrival.

"Don't do that," Mecurio said to Strabidicca, who was about to cut the Jinntar bonds.

"Ha," he sneered. But before his hand had a chance to work a blade through the cord, he froze still in Mercurio's golden beam.

There was a huge gasp of terror that rose from the throats of the Istarim. In confusion and horror, they turned their horses round and galloped madly off into the forest. It would be a long time before they menaced the Mona people again. Mercurio landed. William got off his back.

"My people," Arob said. "The Golden One is our friend. Come, let us greet him."

The gates were opened. Arob, with Emma, led his people to Mercurio and William; who were standing near the captured Jinntars.

As soon as they were close, Emma ran up and embraced her brother.

"Thank goodness you're safe, Emms," he said.

"I'm so pleased to see you again," Emma smiled.

"Listen, buffo. You have me to thank for that," the case stressed.

No one listened except Arob, who swallowed uneasily. The case's voice reminded him that he had broken his promise to Mercurio.

"It is as you said," Mercurio said to William, "Arob has opened the case."

"Oh, crimney," William sighed. "The case always gets its own way."

"Gabbeldy-goop," snapped the case. "I just hope that you see now that all your efforts to return me were for nothing, frazzle-features."

"Now listen here," William began crossly, but just then, there was a snap of a cord. Rogg had cut his bonds with Strabidicca's fallen sword.

"Sooo," Rogg hissed bitterly, "now you meet your fate, Mercurio Nine." He had taken up his power-rod in the one hand he had remaining. Some of the Mona people moved closer to attack.

"Move away, unless you want to become ashes," Rogg said with deep menace.

"Have no dread," Mercurio reassured them. "You never learn, do you Rogg?" There was a high-pitched whistle. The next thing William saw was that Rogg's rod had vanished and the Jinntar was trapped inside three bands of sizzling golden energy. However, with this, Strabidicca ceased glowing. "Out of my way!" he yelled. He pushed his way out and ran to the forest. Several bows were levelled at him.

"Let him go," Arob commanded. "He won't bother us again. He is harmless."

"Harmless! Think so?" the case said quizzically. "Men are not always what they appear, but seldom better."

Little did Arob guess that in the future he would indeed regret having let Stabidicca go free; but that, as they say, is another story.

"Have you found my craft, Star Guard?" Grimston gurgled, fighting to keep the tone of defeat out of his voice, as he thought of all his precious tin that was on board it.

"Your ship can no longer harm this planet; it has become part of it," Mercurio said. "The matter transformer changed it to soil. Soon, grass will grow on it and no one will be able to tell it from any other hill or earthwork."

Rogg spoke a curse in his native tongue, which, although no one except Mercurio could understand, revealed the full look of despair in his face. He then fell into a heavy silence.

"Now, I must take these captives to Belaqua Beta." Mercurio gave a long whistle. From nowhere, a huge golden ball filled the sky.

"Have no dread," Mercurio reassured, "that is but my

spacecraft. I must depart."

"Wait," William said earnestly. He turned to Arob. "You must give the Prize back to Mercurio."

"Butt out, buffo," the case snapped, "I'm Arob's"

"Yes. Mine," Arob said defensively.

"Oh, and by the by, toady-snappers." the case said, "You cannot wish yourselves back to your time since I am now in the hands of the First-Given, as you desired. Yes, I have decided that we shall all stay here."

"You beastly box," Emma cried.

"You can't do that." William stared horrified at the case.

"I'm afraid the Prize has been opened and has thus the right to make the First-Given its permanent owner," Mercurio said. "And since I have never used it as a Prize, it will not grant any of my wishes."

"But you....you don't understand," Emma pleaded. "We've done so much to get it here."

"Yes," William agreed, "it's not right. The case disrupts everything. All I wanted to do was to return it. Everything has gotten so out of hand."

"Our of *your* hands, dumbo," the case chortled. "You should have taken my advice and stayed home."

"Oh, yes! With Benjamin the ghost and you wrecking our lives," William snapped vehemently. "Oh, please make Arob give back the Prize, Mercurio."

"I understand your point of view," replied the golden giant. "But, I'm afraid that the only course of action that I can see, since Arob obviously doesn't wish to give back the Prize, is for you to take the matter up with Jovian."

"Jovian?" William said. "Who's Jovian?"

"The Prize-Maker of Theomodor. He has all the blueprints of the Prizes. I'm sure that if there is something wrong with this model, he will be the one to pin-point it."

"Nothing's wrong with me!" snapped the case.

"But, how can we reach this....this Jovian?" William

asked, rather confused.

"Oh, I can drop you off. I pass Theomodor on my way to Belaqua Beta where I shall deliver my captives to the Salurion Council to stand trial."

There were hisses of hatred and frustration from the trapped Jinntars. Though many a smile lit the faces of the Mona people.

"Well," William pondered. "I suppose that *is* the only way."

"Wait," the case urged in a friendlier tone, thinking what Jovian might do. "Look, buffo, I've changed my mind. If you like I will return us to your time."

"No way," William said adamantly. "I'm going to sort you out, once and for all."

Arob turned to his people, "I will not let Pentrigan Naq's memory perish," he declared. "Rest assured, our people shall be great once more. I have learnt much. We shall rebuild our villages and raise our towers once more. The Mona are the lords of this land. Alfgar of Barrowship taught me much. I feel his knowledge growing already more and more inside me."

"But," he added, "we have also been given a sign of our victory. A symbol of destiny. This is our salvation." He held up the case.

"Quite right too," it agreed. There was a cheer from the crowd.

"Arob," William pleaded, "you mustn't use that case anymore."

But his words fell like silence on Arob, not affecting him at all.

"Do not worry," Arob said haughtily, "you are brave as is your sister, but I am Chieftain now and I know that this is our future; our salvation Prize."

"More like a booby Prize!" Emma retorted.

"If we want your opinion, blabber-mouth," snapped the case, "we'll ask for it." The way the case said this made Emma

125

think that if it had had a tongue it would have stuck it out at her. So she stuck hers out at it.

It was rapidly getting dark. Dusk fell as night sounds came from the forest all around. The moon shone bright with a vague halo around it.

Mercurio gave one long whistle and the Jinntars disappeared in the beam of golden light that shot up into the brig of the round spacecraft.

"Farewell," Mercurio said. But before William could ask what exactly was happening, Mercurio gave another three short, sharp whistles and the two children found themselves inside the fabulous craft.

Mercurio gave three short, sharp whistles and the two children found themselves inside the fabulous craft.

15

An appointment on Theomodor

The ship within was a mass of lights of all colours. They shone subtly, not affecting the children's sight in any way.

Suddenly, from Mercurio's circling ring, came three notes: short, long, short. Immediately the lights all grew brighter, seeming to merge to form one overall colour, the like of which the children had never seen and afterward would never quite be able to explain. In front of them, like the iris of an eye, there opened up a perfectly spherically window. It only stopped when it had taken up a whole section of the ship from floor to ceiling.

It didn't seem as though they were moving at all, but through the large round window, they could see thousands of sparkling stars whisk and twinkle past, like bright white marbles speeding across a black velvet cloth.

"My! We are going fast!" Emma said, finding some words at last.

"Ten parsecs per nanosecond of micro-dotted time," Mercurio replied in a very relaxed voice.

"Will it be long before we reach Theomodor?" William asked.

"Why, no time at all!" And a sound like a songbird's warble came from his halo. Three seats appeared. They seemed to be made of solid light of the same unknown colour as the rest of the inside of the ship's control room.

They all sat down.

"Well, what shall we talk about?" Mercurio began, "I usually have so few people to converse with."

"Except criminals!" William said, rather too bluntly, he thought afterward.

"Well now, criminal is only a word," Mercurio replied, "a definition like all others, to save the need to really explain. What is evil really, but good twisted and tormented by its own hunger and thirst. The Star Guard Code is 'Seek not Revenge, but Reform.' Yes, indeed."

"You must have seen many wonderful things," Emma said thoughtfully.

"I have been to the edge of eternity and back again, little one, observing countless solar systems and many galaxies. Why, just recently I visited the planet Arborus Floria. There, the Loreliums, a highly advanced race of mobile planets, dominate the backward, docile humanoids."

"Humanoids!" William said. "You mean people?"

"Well, almost."

"What are they like?" Emma asked.

"There are three species. One type, the Duartha, are a cross between what you might call horses and men; these the Loreliums ride. Another, the Paddathas, have six arms and four legs; these the Loreliums use as a workforce. And the third the Yumathas, are half-pig and half-human, these the Loreliums eat."

"Ugh, how horrid," Emma gasped.

"Why," Mercurio replied. "Don't you eat meat?"

"Well, yes," Emma confessed, though she would never approach pork in quite the same way again!

"Anyway, a Lorelium – Privet Hedger – was attempting to build a space ship, which is strictly forbidden in that sector. So, I had to destroy the machine and confiscate his memory of its construction. A simple, painless process."

128

"Why is it forbidden?" William asked.

"Oh, the Council have their reasons," Mercurio replied. "The space ways are crowded enough as it is without adding any more difficulties; and also there is a feared atom shortage in that Galaxy."

This had William completely baffle. He decided to just listen.

"In another Galaxy – Tellar Noirus," Mercurio continued, "only one planet supports life but is, in fact, alive itself. It is a single living, thinking thing. It has existed for billions of years in one orbit. But, Zodion grew lonely. Once it created certain forms of life on its surface. They were more or less in its own likeness; tiny versions of the planet itself that could move, work, and breed. The Zodinians worshiped their creator – the planet. Then, they gradually began to create religions of their own and Zodionism went out of fashion. One group even lost faith in everything and became self-questioning skeptics and cynics. The other Zodinions resented this and persecuted them. This led to war. After, every Zodinion surviving believed in the Great Zodion once more. But after a million years or so and more wars, Zodion grew bored with its creations, for they were only increasingly emphasising its own loneliness. During the final war, Zodion let its race of Zodinions destroy themselves completely so that it could be on its own again.

"Anyway, I was called in because Zodion was becoming terribly depressed and was attempting to go out of orbit to try to find a new friend. That would have disturbed the natural order of things as well as involving a great deal of paperwork for the Salurian Council to balance the books. I set it right, therefore."

"How?" Emma attempted to keep a note of total disbelief out of her voice.

"Quite simply. I asked the Extreme Mandrot of Sector Twelve to fashion a conscious, talking moon for me. This, I set into orbit around Zidion. Now Zidion is as happy as a Stellar Fairy, talking with the moon about such things as 'If I am I because you are you, and if you are you because I am I; then I am not and you are not you.'"

William couldn't bring himself to ask what a Stellar Fairy was!

"On another planet," Mercurio continued, enjoying his reminiscences, "in Sector Seven, called Aurora Alpha, Crystalline Forms shimmer in the pink and green light of the many moons surrounding it. These Crystalline Forms don't move but change shape from time to time. They communicate with each other by sending resounding tinkles through the atmosphere. The Fire Creatures of Ingitall Three were taking the Tinklers, as the Crystal beings are nicknamed, home for their young as toys. It was not a criminal offense although the Tinklers often pined away as soon as they were removed from their home planet, for the Fire Creatures hadn't realised that the Tinklers were living beings. Despite an occasional flare-up, the Ingitalls abide by the Salurion Law, so it didn't take long to set matters straight."

There was a pause. Then, "What was your most difficult case?" William asked.

"Ah-ha, that was eons ago, when I was a young cadet. My trainer was Adonio Five. Now, on the planet Bennor Ciss, only two creatures lived: Belbos and Cunifor. I suppose you would call them deities, though strictly of the second rank! They were constantly at war with one another. The energy they released during combat gave heat and light to two neighbouring planets: Treamor and Reamor. These planets were both inhabited by two races of flying Butterfly Creatures. They worshiped Belbos and Cunifor as their life-giving gods, as indeed they were.

"Then, three eons ago, for some reason best known to themselves, they stopped fighting and merged together to form one being, Belcun. Thus, the war ended and peace took

130

away the light and heat from Treamor and Reamor. The Butterfly Creatures mostly faded into the soft shadows and dispersed into the winds of Time, though some, cursing their traitor gods, went underground. In time, they lost their wings, gaining claws and sharp teeth. They became savage creatures of the night, fighting and feeding; feeding and fighting.

"Then, two eons ago, after the Star Guard had failed to persuade Becun to split into Cunifor and Belbos again, Belcun decided to leave Gennor Ciss, devouring Treamor and Reamor as he did so. He roamed the galaxy. Peace had destroyed his natural balance; the concept of power obsessed him. He devoured planets and then whole solar systems. No single Star Guard could stop Belcun, for his power was not that of a first-rank deity. Adonio Five attempted to trick Belcun into a trap he had set but Belcun could see most things and dropped poor Adonio into the abyss of nothingness that exists in the middle of the next universe.

"It took the entire Star Guard, mustering their power together, to trap Belcun. But he wouldn't be taken. He surrendered himself into billions of round, black pieces. To this very day, these black balls or holes drift through the universe devouring light and gravity and planets. Naturally, when a Star Guard sees one he eliminates it, but there are so many that we cannot afford the time to hunt them all. Besides, the Council has taken them into consideration; put them down in their books, so that now they are often necessary to maintain the Council's established order."

"It sounds an awful place out there," William said nodding towards the stars. Emma agreed.

"Awful, no," Mercurio answered. "Difficult, why of course! But there are so many beautiful things in this universe of ours. That is why the Star Guard was created to protect all planets and life within the Salurian Domain; to maintain the chain of being and balance of order.

"Each galaxy has its own patrol and base planet. The

head of the planet is a Council Member and directs the Star Guards in his, her, or its sector. Naturally, not all Star Guards look the same. In this galaxy, the humanoid form is the norm. In others, as stated, the plant form may be the dominant type; whilst in others, beings made of solid light, or fire, or matter which I could not describe to you, are the norm. In each case, the Star Guards adopt the form that is most suitable."

"All these different names and places. It's all so hard to believe!" William thoughtfully scratched his curly, black hair.

"Oh, the names are merely for convenience. The universe by itself contains no signs, no names. The Council just gave the different worlds names so that the books could be kept straight. Just believe in life in its many varied forms; that is the greatest Prize of all. That is why such worlds as Earth are 'closed' planets. Life on your planet must not be interfered with; it is too primitive, like a child growing. Only when it reaches manhood will the Council make contact and Earth will be opened for visitors. The Jinnatars chief crime is that they attempted to interfere with your race's natural growth."

"And that's why I want to return the case," William stressed. "As you say, our planet is 'closed' and the case, like the Jinntars, is nothing but an interference."

"Yes, do you know that beastly thing almost had me falling from Pentrigan's wooden tower?" Emma complained.

"Those Prizes are so temperamental," Mercurio agreed, "especially 1.B. Prizes for they are over-proud that they aren't 1.C. Prizes, yet intensely jealous of 1.A. Specials. So, they tend to go rather over-the-top when it comes to granting wishes. That is why I never used mine, my friends. You see, although given as awards, they tend to make up their own rules very often and choose whom they wish to own them. So, since Arob Naq was tricked by the Prize into making a wish, he effectively became the First-Given, thus the Prize had power over him as well. Really, I should have been more careful!"

"Well, why couldn't you have taken it from him if you protect planets from outside interference?" William asked earnestly.

"Ah, you see it's in Jovian's contract that no Prize can ever be taken from a First-Given or his descendants; and Jovian is no one to go against. He is a High Member of the Salurian Council and almost as old as the oldest galaxy. I'm afraid his talents are not quite as, um, all embracing as they used to be. His memory is not, well, what it once was. Even a deity is not all-powerful; for he cannot build a wall, which he cannot knock down. Still, even a deity is entitled to be wrong occasionally. As long as he doesn't go kicking aside solar systems or blowing out suns. Actually, I think you will like Jovian, but you must remember to keep him talking or he may forget that you're on Theomodor and that would be unfortunate ....or fortunate – depending on your point of view and love of clocks."

"Unfortunate!" William swallowed uneasily.

"Oh, I shouldn't worry; just remember to keep his attention."

The round craft sped silently through a shining spiral of stars. Tiny barbs of light seemed to explode into enormous planets glowing all colours; some with rings circling round, some with moons and other planets orbiting them. As soon as the worlds came into gigantic view, they shrank and vanished. The effect was like looking through a hypnotic kaleidoscope.

"It shouldn't be more than three divided macro lengths before we reach Theomodoar," Mercurio announced. "Then, I shall go on to deliver Grimston Rogg and his motley crew to the judgment of the Prime Trig on Belaqua Beta."

"What will happen to them?" Emma asked.

"Nothing much," Mercurio replied nonchalantly. "Their memories will be removed and all hostile feeling eliminated. They will then serve a period of time helping different

133

communities and afterwards, they will be returned to Wheebil One. Standard procedure."

"That doesn't sound too bad," William agreed.

"Of course not. The Council does not seek to punish but to pilldreat."

"Pilldreat?" Emma didn't understand (who would!).

"Pilldreat is a reform policy, whereby 'badness' is pulled out and 'goodness' slotted in its place. Simple. Now, I bet you both feel hungry?" Mercurio gave a low, short hum and two orange-silver cups filled with clear liquid appeared in the children's hands. "I think you will find this to your liking," Mercurio said.

Emma, being thirsty, took a cautious sip. Then she drank a mouthful. "Ummm. It's absolutely delicious, Billy. It tastes like strawberries and cream."

William drank some of his. "Crimney, yes! It is scrumptious. But mine tastes like chocolate peppermints; my favourite."

"Wait!" Emma said slightly shocked. "Now mine tastes like lemon candy!"

Mercurio laughed. "Ambrosade will taste like anything nice you want it to. Simply think of any food you like and it will be in your mouth."

He was right, too! To William, the liquid tasted of roast beef and horseradish and then plum pudding as rich as the kind old Martha made. To Emma, it tasted like roast turkey with chestnut and brandy stuffing and then bananas and vanilla ice cream.

After they had finished, both felt exceedingly full and satisfied. The orange-silver cups disappeared immediately after the last drop of ambrosade had been consumed.

Outside, William could see that they had entered a whirling pool of brilliant white stars that formed a sparkling tunnel, which the ship shot through, like a golden bullet from a gleaming barrel.

134

A song percolated through the control room. It was Mercurio's song. Afterward, William tried to remember how the words had gone. It seemed a very long song; quite magically beautiful. But the only words he thought he remembered were these:

A creature sang a song on the edge of night,

Of things he had known when all was bright;
Saying:
Oh, sky that is spun out of the sea,
Keep clear each treasured memory.

Yes, the creature on the edge of night,
Knew that there must be an end to light;
He sang a song of the swift, sweet pain,

Of things that are once,
And never again.

....never again....again....again, the words fell into William's mind like pebbles into water, ripples spreading until they seemed real and solid, and William was that creature on the edge of night and it was his song.

Well, of course. But, of course. William had fallen asleep. So had Emma. Mercurio woke them.

"Oh, look, Billy!"

"Yes, and you too Emms."

Instead of the old tunics they had been wearing, each had on a one-piece suit of dark gold.

"They're beautiful," Emma said.

"And it's good to be clean again," William added. "Thank you."

"My pleasure," Mercurio replied happily. "Well, little friends, we're here."

"Oh, Theomodor!" William suddenly felt anxious. "Are you going to wait for us?"

"No," Mercurio replied.

"Then how will we ever get back?" Emma asked.

"Not only to Earth, but to our own time?" William added.

"Have no dread, don't disturb yourselves," Mercurio reassured. "It will be taken care of. Just don't let Jovian wander off the subject and forget about you. Then, everything will be alright. I have already informed him that you're coming down to see him. I've put a visa through the proper channels. I'll have you down in a parsec."

William and Emma felt rather sad at leaving the friendly Star Guard, but this feeling was overshadowed by apprehension at their appointment with the Prize-Maker.

"Until we meet again, then," Mercurio said.

"Goodbye," the children replied together.

Mercurio's halo gave one long whistle.

16

Well-Buttered Bread and the Prize-Maker

William felt as though he had been in the room a long, long time; in fact for as long as he could recall. Probably his whole life! Everything else, Mercurio, the case, all the other events of the last few days seemed like just a dream. The room was home; he felted that he belonged there.

William looked at the stranger beside him, "Who is she?" he wondered.

It was only when she spoke, saying that the room felt like home to her, that he remembered that this was his sister, Emma, and that the room definitely wasn't home at all!

"What a curious feeling, Emms," William said.

"Yes, about as curious as anything can be!" she replied.

"Well, it seems to be going now, thank goodness." William scratched his head thoughtfully.

The room they were in was cluttered with all sorts of bric-a-brac, of which the vast majority was a great assortment of clocks of all manner of description tick-tick-ticking. In fact, all four of the room's tall walls were lined with dozens and dozens of grandfather clocks placed side by side. They were of all different heights, shapes, and colours and were dominated by the "Granddaddy of them all.' It was twice as wide and large as the others and set grandly in the middle of the wall facing the children. On its face was inscribed '2+2=5. It is later than you think.'

There were also many sculptures of creatures and plants of all descriptions. William could make neither head nor tail of other objects in the room; they were like nothing he had ever seen before. But there were so many that, although the room was very large, there was little space to move because of the clutter.

Looking up, William could see that the entire ceiling appeared to be a map of the stars. It seemed enormous somehow, as if the ceiling was far too big for the walls of the room. William was just about to remark on this peculiar perspective, when-

"Oh, chicken fry, it's not there either!"

"W...who said that?" Emma clutched onto her brother.

"Oh, look." William pointed.

"No one said 'that'! It's rude to point; don't you know that by now?"

The voice belonged to an old man, who walked through one of the grandfather clocks into the room.

"Oh, my!" Emma gasped.

The man was wearing large round steel spectacles that made his eyes look like two big blue balloons. Apart from this, and had he not been dressed in an old and rather crumpled white tweed suit and plus fours, Emma would have thought that he looked just like Father Christmas. He sported a long white beard and moustache and had a very ruddy complexion and a stomach as large as a humpback bridge.

"He looks like Father Christmas," Emma whispered to her brother.

"Learn to think before you speak," the old man said as if he was talking to someone neither of the children could see. "It will profit you; there is so little competition."

There was a sudden round of applause, as if from some

invisible audience.

"Excuse me, sir. We are looking for a Mr. Jovian," William ventured.

"Who said that?" the man blustered, looking straight past the children.

"I did, sir," William replied earnestly.

"So, you did!" The man paused. Suddenly, he was wearing a black top hat and evening clothes and the most enormous red bow tie that William had ever seen. He stepped about ten paces forward until he was eight or nine feet from the children. He peered at them both. Then, making a curious smacking sound with his lips, he said, "Ah, yes, you're Tambort from Splinctre Rombo. I have been expecting you. I see you've brought your pet with you. How nice!" He looked at Emma and offered her what seemed like some sort of dog biscuit.

"How rude!" Emma exclaimed in a very vexed voice.

"No, sir, you misunderstand," William said as quickly as he could. "I am William Whipper -Snapper from Earth and this is my sis...."

"Do not worry that you are misunderstood. Concern yourself rather that you misunderstand others," Jovian interrupted. "Now, ah, yes! Someone told me about you, though for the life of me I cannot remember whom. Still, I must have your visa around here somewhere." He scratched his head of hair that sprouted like long white grass from his head. He was no longer wearing a top hat or evening clothes, but a long red velvet smoking gown and silver slippers. He rootled in several places, but came up with nothing."

"Well, never mind," he said. "Earth, you say? Ah, there it is; quite an insignificant place!"

William and Emma gazed up to where Jovian was staring. On the map on the ceiling, they could see a tiny speck moving from deep in the map towards the front. This picture of the Earth was growing visibly until it was all that filled the ceiling. If it was a picture; for it appeared to be moving, albeit ever so slowly. William could tell it was the Earth because he recognised the outline of the British Isles.

"Ah, yes," Jovian said, pleased with himself and the Earth sped back into the invisible distance like a stone disappearing into a dark, deep pond. The map of the stars took its place once more.

"Crimney, what a curious map!" William said.

"Map!" Jovian chuckled. "Why, my dear Tambort, that's no map. That's Section Six of the Universe. Ha, ha! You see the ceiling is like the glass of a microscope, only reversed." He waved his hand nonchalantly. "One of my minor miracles."

There was a loud round of applause from the invisible audience.

"Sir, we came about the case," William attempted to get to the point.

"Case? What case?"

"The 1.B. Prize!"

"Oh, the 1.B. Prize," Jovian muttered rather blankly. He promptly went over and began fiddling with the mechanism of one of his grandfather clocks.

"Yes, sir, the Prize," William persisted.

"Ah, the Prize. Why didn't you say so!" Jovian turned so suddenly that Emma jumped. He was wearing a long silver coat with ridiculously wide lapels. "Yes, of course; you want one. Well, um, I know you have a visa. So, who nominated you and when and where and why and…."

"No, sir," William said firmly, "we don't *want* a Prize. We want to *give* one back."

"Give one back!" Jovian wagged his head. "Oh, dear! Oh, dear! Can't have that. Really can't! Sorry, not at all. Give one back indeed! Once you receive a Prize, it's yours for life. Didn't bother reading the contract I suppose? Give one back indeed! It would jumble all the book, all…..all the books." Still shaking his head, he went back to fiddling with the clock.

140

Opening its dark green case, he gave the pendulum a sharp tug. Immediately, the room was filled with loud music, like that of a large military brass band, playing Latin-American music.

"Si senora. Its-a now tena microsecondsa squarda," the clock boomed.

"No, no, no! You're still slow," Jovian angrily slammed the case shut. The music went reeling off-key and stopped.

The two children looked at each other, bewildered.

"I don't believe he's a deity at all," Emma said. She was beginning to feel very fed up with the whole 'adventure.'

"Oh, still here are we?" Jovian said, turning to eye the children. "Soooo, what can I do for you now?" he said somewhat testily. He was wearing blue denim jeans and a pink T-shirt with 'Jovian Rules, O.K.' written on it.

"Please, sir, the Prize causes nothing but trouble all the time; it's useless," William urged, trying to keep a faint note of despair out of his voice.

"Causes trouble all the time, you say Tambort? Well, if time doesn't work things out, at least it makes them more acceptable as my old grandfather clock used to say. Yes, the worst things never happen."

"What's he talking about?" Emma pouted her mouth in a vexed fashion.

"This is becoming more and more unreal." William shook his head. He was beginning to feel stiff all over.

"Stretch reality far enough and you can see right through it," Jovian commented. He was wearing a chef's outfit – enormous upright hat and all. Except, instead of being white the uniform seemed to be one large picture of a chef wearing an outfit that appeared to be a picture of a chef wearing an outfit that appeared to be a picture of… well and so on; a picture within a picture within a picture. Except for this instance, all the pictures appeared to move; very confusing!

Jovian went over to a table, which was in the shape of one large flower, its open petals being the tabletop. From what appeared to be a large vase with water designs on it, Jovian produced a huge chunk of bread, a golden knife, and an enormous mound of butter; all neatly arranged on a plate that looked exactly like a giant bumblebee.

Emma began to feel hungry again.

"I like to butter my bread with plenty of butter," Jovian said in a singsong voice. "Yes, I do. Oh, yes, I do." Jovian put all the butter on the bread so that in the end it was of the same thickness as the bread.

"How wasteful!" Emma exclaimed.

"Only the ignorant know everything." There were cheers as Jovian ate the whole lot in two enormous bites; his mouth expanding like a snake's to swallow his meal. There was a burst of applause, then silence.

"No wonder he's so fat," Emma said to her brother rather loudly. "If he fell out of bed he'd rock himself to sleep."

But William didn't feel like saying anything at all. He didn't even feel himself. It was hard to explain, but he felt incredibly stiff, almost as if his limbs were turning to wood. He was beginning to see a clock dial, not just in front of his eyes, but attached to his eyes and face; a part of him, in fact. He could hear the invisible audience laughing at him and other grandfather clocks were saying, 'Resist, resist. It's not too bad being a clock, but it's not too good, either.'

He caught a glimpse of Emma out of the corner of his rigid eye. She was fading, shimmering as if she was drifting away and would vanish soon to somewhere else. Then, he remembered Mercurio's warning and he understood. He shivered for he knew that he was changing into a grandfather clock; for he had lost Jovian's attention. The invisible audience said, 'Give in, give in,' the other clocks said, 'Resist, resist.'

William tried to flex all his muscles, shake himself out of it, as when you're in bed after sleeping and, although your eyes are open, you cannot move any part of your body at all. William struggled, mustering every last iota of strength that was draining away, to move the muscles in his mouth to get at least one word out. Then, with one last great effort:

"But your Prize should never have been given in the first place!!!" William shouted at the top of his voice. It was like breaking some magic spell. He felt perfectly normal once again.

"Noisy, aren't we?" Jovian said, rubbing his nose with a large, crumpled handkerchief that had a picture of a nose on it. The picture of the nose sneezed, "Gerzunteeeee."

"Bless you," Jovian said and put the handkerchief in his sporran again, which was part of the Scottish Highland Officer's uniform he was wearing now.

"Most inconvenient!" He eyed Emma suspiciously. "Oh well, Tambort. I suppose you had best explain. But do try to keep your pet quiet!"

"I am NOT a pet," Emma said vehemently. Jovian ignored her.

"Well, the Prize....." William began.

"Be brief," Jovian interrupted. "I have a 1.A. Prize to prepare for Sentinor Seven, son of Graptiinor Three, Salurian Law-Giver for Section Two. It's Sentinor's Incubation Day Celebration. He gave his girlfriend hungry Lilies; she's not his girlfriend anymore!" He stopped suddenly, as if he had forgotten what he was going to say.

"Well, sir," William began quickly. "It's very important that you take the Prize back because..."

"Don't interrupt!" Jovian glared at him. He paused. "Well?" He looked impatiently at William. "Are you going to explain about the Prize or not, Tambort?"

"Yes," William said firmly. "As I was going to say, it was given to Arob Naq by mistake. He never had a contract with you. You see the Prize just doesn't work for Earth people, perhaps because Earth is a 'closed' planet and so should have

143

no outside interference. The Prize *is* one, and...and well, there is something wrong with it."

"Wrong!" Jovian boomed. His glasses misted up. Immediately, two tiny windscreen wipers appeared, cleaned them, and vanished. "No, no, no, that's impossible. No Prize of mine ever malfunctions."

"But, sir!"

There was a sudden sound of booing.

"But, sir," William carried on regardless, "that may be so here, however, Earth is a 'closed' planet and the fact that the Prize was given by mistake and without a Contract is surely against Council rules; they might even say that....that you cooked the books!" The booing ceased, with an astonished gasp.

"Cooked the books!" Jovian trembled. William thought that he might have gone just a little too far. "Cooked the books! What do you think I am? A Woodsquelcher from Zipsee! I've never eaten words in my life, not even my own."

"Why don't you bring the Prize back here and see for yourself," Emma said bluntly.

"Yes," William agreed.

"Oh, alright, alright," Jovian moaned. "Anything for a little peace. You're worse than the talking Metal Trees of Arburison; yap, yap, yap all the time."

Jovian went over to a bright blue grandfather clock. He opened the glass clock face. "Prize 1.B., co-ordinates Earth 3, Solar System 398 dash **2**. Come in, your time is up."

"Gotcha, fella. Ten-four, little buddy, ten four," the clock said as a mass choir hummed 'Yankee Doodle Dandy.' Suddenly the room was lit by a flash of purple light. In a flurry of sparks that were coloured with stars and stripes, the Prize appeared on the table – with a picture of a table on it. The humming stopped with the boom of a cannon.

"Really, clock. I wish you wouldn't overdo it," Jovian muttered.

"You wanted me?" the Prize said somewhat testily. "May I inquire as to what these two oil-slicks have been saying?"

"How have you been functioning?" Jovian asked.

"Very, very, very, very, very, very, very, very well," the case said decisively and, adding for good measure, "as all first-class 1.B. Prizes should after the expert way you make them. Yes, I'm alright."

"You're half-left," William said. "What about Benjamin and our croquet lawn?"

"And all the other troubles you've caused," Emma added.

"You're not going to believe these two grumpy bears, are you?" the case said indignantly.

"I'll just inspect your Perry Wonker." Jovian opened the case; its purple light bathed his face. He made a sucking sound and swallowed the light so that none was left inside the case. He hiccupped. Three purple bubbles floated up from his mouth and burst in a fluster of mauve light just above his head.

Suddenly, there was the sound of a huge wild animal roaring in a charge and the sound of hundreds of people screaming with fear. Emma clung onto her brother.

"Oh, dear!" Jovian said, taking out his pink half-hunter watch, from which the sound was coming. It stopped immediately and the watch proclaimed, "It's getting late, it's getting late; light bends, time curves, waiting ends. It's twelve macro lengths minus eight."

"Oh, dear. Oh, dear!" Jovian put the watch away in the pocket of his yellow tuxedo, which he now wore with a 'matching' pair of bright orange trousers. "I'm expecting the Extreme Mandrot of the Salurian Council for supper. I've got some clocks cooking; she loves every minute. She never, ever wastes anybody's time!"

The mention of cooking clocks, considering how close

he came to becoming one, made William rather uneasy. "What about the Prize?" the boy asked.

"May your days be lank and your life be flat, buffo," the case snapped.

"I'll return it to you when I've checked its central Somniscope, diversified its Droopsifier, and gyrated its Domwangler," Jovian reassured him.

"I feel like a crocodile in a handbag factory," the case said with bitter irony.

"No," William urged. "We don't want the Prize back. Thank you, very much, sir!"

"Killjoy!" the case said resentfully.

"Ah, well, Tambort. Then I suppose you can trundle off," Jovian said. "I shall put down a note against the Prize in my register and arrange a refund."

"But how are we going to get back?" Emma asked excitedly.

"Yes, and now you have the Prize," William began, "and Arob Naq hasn't. That means it will never be passed on and it won't be found by me or anyone else! So won't the future be altered now that the case can no longer interfere? Won't our fates be changed?"

"No, no, no, of course not!" Jovian reassured them. "I'll arrange everything. Everyone harmed will be okey-coakey once more. Besides," he waved his hands nonchalantly, "what men commonly call their fate is mostly their own foolishness."

There was a loud round of applause.

"Do let's go home, Billy," Emma said. "I'm ever so tired and hungry and fed up with being mistaken for your pet." And who could blame her? After all, nothing is so commonplace as the miraculous once you get used to it.

"But how, Emms? How can we return?"

"Oh, no trouble Tambort. I'll merely adjust the Universal Gap-Bridging Sprocket to your co-ordinates, then

146

send you back through a wrinkle in time and a crease in space to exactly when and where you started from. Now, let me see." Jovian went over the largest grandfather clock and opened its face; '2+2=5. It's later than you think' inscribed on it. Beneath, were symbols and names that William didn't recognise as well as the vague outline of a face; half-happy, half-sad.

"Ah, yes. Earth 3 Solar System 398 2 (squared). Time 1880. Sol. Spec. 487 dash n. England. Frum by Tzam Orita." Jovian paused. "Hum," he contemplated, as a Father Christmas outfit replaced what he was wearing before. "I think I shall have a quick slice of bread and butter before the Extreme Mandrot arrives. I will have to get ready for my deliveries after."

"He *is* Father Christmas!" Emma exclaimed. But her words were distant. Jovian proceed to butter thickly an enormous chunk of bread.

"Goodbye, sir," William said.

"Who said that?" Jovian exclaimed, looking straight through them.

"Oh, well, hey-ho," the case said. "From now on, I'm thinking only of me."

A sound of laughter. Then, a sound of far-off trumpets that were rather off-key. Then, the loud 'twang' of a spring; a round of applause and everything went as blank as butter, except for the ceiling which grew and grew until the children seemed to be in the middle of it with no sign whatsoever of the rest of the room.

They could see the Earth in front of them, from out of a sea of sparkling stars and darkness, getting larger and larger; nearer and nearer. Then, they saw the outline of the British Isles. They entered some clouds and the next thing they knew they were halfway up a large horse chestnut tree in the middle of a snow-covered dell.

Jovian went over to a bright blue grandfather clock.

17

How It All Ended

Together, they walked towards their home; a mile away from where they had 'landed.' The sky was a deep, night blue, made milky by soft snow starting to gently flutter and fall.

"Goodness, Emms, just look over there!" William suddenly stopped. "The old oak tree is still standing and the summer house is intact; good as new. Something has changed, despite what Jovian said."

"Oh, never mind, Billy," Emma yawned, rubbing a weary eye. "I'm too tired and hungry to bother with it."

As they walked into their house wearing their ordinary clothes once more, it was almost as if nothing had ever happened.

"Ah, the wanderers return," said a familiar voice as they entered the hall, wiping the snow off their boots. "Really, you know you've been out for a lot longer than you said you would." It was their mother who came out of the drawing room. She began helping Emma off with her coat. William put his coat on the stand. Everything looked alarmingly normal.

Their mother didn't seem in the least surprised to see them, after what William considered to be at least two days' absence. He decided that Jovian must have been more skillful at returning them than he had thought.

"Where did you go then?" she asked as they followed

her in.

"You wouldn't believe it," Emma began, not realising what she was saying.

"Yes, Mama," William interrupted hastily. "We went all the way over to Jack's Dell and climbed in the trees."

"With all this snow! My, you two are adventurous," said their mother laughing.

William and Emma gave each other a knowing smile.

"Now, your Papa has gone to see Miss Trelor Diddermouse about her knees," their mother announced. "So, you two just come in and eat. Then, you can go straight off to bed. As Thomas Jefferson said: '*I like dreams of the future better than history of the past,*' *so,* you'll want to be up early tomorrow."

"Why, Mama?" William asked.

"Now don't be silly, William. You know as well as I do that it's Christmas day tomorrow." His mother ruffled his hair affectionately.

"Oh, of course!" William realised that they had been away, in fact, for more than two days.

As they sat down at the supper table, William half-expected Benjamin to come stumbling through the wall. But he didn't. *I wonder if he got his Chains in the end?* William thought; though somehow, he knew that he had.

Later, William gazed through his bedroom window at sarabands of snow twirling in the darkness. Outside, an owl seemed to call down, 'Look, cold night. Look, cold night,' and there were dark outlines of the trees, huddled together against the chill winter wind as stars were occasionally seen sparking brightly above.

Rather hazy-eyed, William crept into bed. He puffed up his pillow and lay back, thinking of the extraordinary events of the past few days. It seemed as though he was viewing them through a telescope that was the wrong way around. The more he thought of them, the more removed they appeared to be; untouchable and distant as dreams do, when you are suddenly woken at cock-crow.

Despite their mother saying that they would want to be up early, both William and Emma woke up rather late on Christmas morning. They got dressed quickly and came down together.

They saw Walters looking uncommonly cheerful. She had returned, or perhaps she had never left in the first place!

Both their parents were waiting for them in front of the tall, brightly decorated Christmas tree; as the large log fire burnt merrily in the grate.

William could hear the bells from the village church ringing out in angular voices of joy of Yuletide. Indeed, the happiness seemed to have come through with the sound and settled in the house; Dr. Whipper-Snapper had the largest smile on his face. Neither of his children had ever witnessed such an expansive grin before.

"Ah, children," he declared, "joy of the season to you, my dears."

"Happy Christmas," their mother added, coming forward and kissing them both. All the bad feelings of the past seemed to have vanished as quickly as a wish.

"Happy Christmas, Papa, Mama." They hugged their parents in turn. William felt something, almost indefinable, had changed for the better.

"Children, your Papa and I have a surprise for you," their mother announced.

"Yes," Dr. Whipper-Snapper nodded happily. "We have come into a considerable sum of money. It was left us, apparently, by some relation of ours; a certain Mr. Jovian. Though I must admit I have never heard of him before. Anyway, it was in lieu of something that a certain Mr. Tambort, representing our family, gave back to him."

The children looked at each other in amazement.

"Anyhow, you two," their mother said, "just look

151

outside."

The two children went, slightly apprehensively, over to the French window. Both gazed out wide-eyed to where Old Tom was holding a white horse and a white pony.

"For us?" Emma asked in disbelief.

"Yes, my dears. The horse is for William, the pony for you," Dr. Whipper-Snapper said. "I consider that it is about time that you both learnt to ride properly. See more of the things around you. Get out more."

"It's just… just, crimney!"

And together, William and Emma started joyfully laughing and laughing and laughing at the top of their voices.

Both the children gazed out wide-eyed, through the window, at a white horse and a white pony.

18

PS....?

Well, that is the story of The Strange Case of William Whipper-Snapper and that is how it all ended. I hope that you found it as enjoyable in the reading as I did in the telling of it. But, I can hear you ask: "Oh, how can you possibly say that it was a *true* story?"

A very good point indeed! As someone once said – I cannot remember whom! - "The truth will set you free, but first, it will mess with your mind!"

However, as I said before, I heard all of this from someone whom I have no reason to doubt. Actually, if truth were told, it was not so much from a person, as from a 'thing.' Yes, I heard the story from this little silver case that I found in my back garden, you see, and ever since, ever since; well, ha-ha, who can tell when it ever really is....

.... The End?

From the silence of stars,
Where dreams belong,
Past the whispering Moon,
Comes tomorrow the tune,
And Fresh Hope its newly sung song.

I heard this story from this little silver
case that I found in my back garden.

David R. Morgan

David R Morgan lives in England. He is a full-time teacher and writer. He has written music journalism, poetry, and children's books. He has won awards for his writing; both for fiction and poetry. For the last 5 years, he has been working on the Soundings Project with his son, Toby, performing his own poetry/writing to Toby's original music and their self-created video/films. This work is on YouTube, Spotify and Soundcloud.

For over a year, he has been working with Terrie Sizemore and her innovative Florida, USA Publishing House A2Z Press LLC, writing a variety of picture/story books. It has been an exhilarating experience, which has now led to the revision and republishing of his acclaimed 1982 novel: *The Strange Case of William Whipper-Snapper*. This is what you now have in your hands. Please do take your first steps along the magical road that William and his sister, Emma open the door to. Who knows where it may lead! Come on, one foot in front of the other and ... off we go ....red sky at night, shepherd's delight. Blue sky at night, day.

ACKNOWLEDGMENTS

I would also like to give a special thank you to Terrie Sizemore for all her incredible hard work in preparing this book for publication.

Lightning Source UK Ltd.
Milton Keynes UK
UKHW011828150321
380381UK00001B/285